Her Private Chef

Lynn Story

Copyright © 2021 by **Lynn Story**

All rights reserved. No part of this publication may be reproduced, distributed or transmitted in any form or by any means, without prior written permission.

Lynn Story

www.stitchesandstories.com

Publisher's Note: This is a work of fiction. Names, characters, places, and incidents are a product of the author's imagination. Locales and public names are sometimes used for atmospheric purposes. Any resemblance to actual people, living or dead, or to businesses, companies, events, institutions, or locales is completely coincidental.

Lynn Story, Hampton, Virginia

Her Private Chef/ Lynn Story—1st ed.

To Larry, with love

Chapter 1
Sarah

When I was a little girl dreaming of the day, I would marry prince charming; I never imagined a spring wedding. In my mind, fall was the perfect time of year. The weather would cool, nature providing a vast array of colors. I would have a crown of vibrantly colored leaves in contrast to my white dress.

But it wasn't my wedding I was planning on this cold cloudy day in March. I was helping to plan a wedding for my boss and friend, Eryn Upton, who was getting married in April, and we had only a month left to complete all the details to ensure her special day was magical. I suppose a more optimistic person would say that March is the perfect time to plan a wedding as a distraction from the winter blues. But even April could be cold here in southeast Virginia. I remember one Easter as a child we had snow. Eryn wanted a spring wedding, not because she had romantic notions of it representing a fresh awakening, rebirth, or hope of better days to come. She was practical and the owner of a garden center. Spring and summer are her busiest time of year. April was the latest she could go on a honeymoon, otherwise, they would have to wait until the next winter. Neither Eryn nor her fiancé, Blue, were willing to wait.

We divided the job of planning the wedding between myself and Eryn's best friend, Penelope Curtis. Penn is in charge of the ceremony and the dresses, a perfect job for a fashion designer with her own boutique here in town. I am in charge of the reception. Both Eryn and Penn have helped me through one of the worst moments of my life, when my stalker ex-coworker kidnapped Eryn to get my attention, so agreeing to help plan her wedding seemed like the least I could do. When Penn assigned the reception to me, she said it would be easy since the reception was being held at the restaurant owned and operated by Blue's best friend Chuck Thomas. Chuck and his staff would handle most of the work I just needed to pick the menu. That seemed like a simple enough task, but it had taken a month to agree on light fare rather than a full-on three-course meal; Chuck loves to cook, and he is all about feeding people. I finally reasoned with him that Eryn and Blue were going to be eager to start their honeymoon and would not care about the food, anyway. By the look he gave me, perhaps that wasn't the thing to say to a chef. I'm sure he sees this as an opportunity to showcase his best dishes and hopefully add to his customer base. I can understand that it is a perfect opportunity, and it makes good business sense to attract new customers with a captive audience, but realistically how many people want a heavy meal at a wedding reception? They want to party, drink, and toast the bride and groom.

I shouldn't complain. Penn has tasked herself with the ceremony itself and designing the wedding gown and bridesmaid's dresses. She is the owner of Honeysuckle Lane, a boutique that showcases her own designs and a carefully curated collection from other designers.

It had been a long week at the garden center; reception planning notwithstanding; it was Friday. I want to go home and veg out.

I was changing into something suitable for a date with my TV when my phone rang with a very familiar ring tone.

"Hello, Penn."

"What are you doing tonight?"

"I have a full schedule of eating microwave junk food and watching old movies."

"Oh, my god! Please tell me you're joking."

I sighed loudly; I don't think Penn has ever eaten anything from a microwave.

"No, I'm not joking. You haven't lived until you have eaten pizza rolls and drank a half-gallon of chocolate milk," I tell her.

"I'm going to get Eryn and we're having an intervention!" She clicks off before I can respond. I plop down on my bed because I realize she isn't joking. I hurry and finish changing before she arrives. I pray that if I'm already in my yoga pants and t-shirt, she won't suggest going out. The doorbell rings.

"Hi Penn, come on in."

"Oh my god, it's worse than I expected." She says, taking one glimpse of me.

I looked out my door, "Where's Eryn?"

"Working, where else?"

Penn looks around the room as if a pizza roll might jump out at her. She had an armload of magazines.

I jokingly ask, "So, you're a one-woman intervention?"

"If you want something done right.... I've ordered ramen it should be here soon. I hoped we can search through some of these, and you could give me your opinion on the flowers."

"Shouldn't you be asking Eryn about the flowers; she's the horticulturist."

"True, but I can't have her planning her own wedding and besides, you work with her, you can help."

"Penn, I'm a bookkeeper and I help in the retail shop; I know nothing about the plants."

"You sell them, that's close enough."

I know there is no arguing with her, I give in and join her on the sofa. "Okay, let's see what you have."

"Great!" Penn settles spreading the magazines out on the coffee table.

"Now, I was considering a spring mix for the centerpieces. What are your thoughts on Calla Lilies for the bouquet?"

"I believe you should ask Eryn this."

"She is going to tell me it doesn't matter."

I nod. That is true. Eryn would be happier just eloping with Blue and not having a big wedding. However, once Penn puts her mind to something, there is no stopping her.

There was a knock at the door.

"Here's some cash for a tip, I already paid." Penn fishes some bills out of her purse.

The delivery person hands me a grocery bag full of food.

"How much did you order?" I ask, carrying the food into the kitchen.

"I wasn't sure how hungry you were, so I ordered extra everything."

I shake my head. Penn does everything big. I swear she invented the phrase "go big or go home".

She and I sit on the floor eating ramen and pouring over the magazines. Penn brought her project binder out and started making notes. She is famous for her binders. She makes a new binder each time she is designing something new, but she bought a special one for Eryn's wedding. It's stuffed full of lists, charts, ideas, sketches and you name it is in Penn's project binder.

"Where are your notes?" She asks. Penn insists I take notes about the food options I discuss with Chuck and my impressions when tasting the samples.

"Oh, they are around here somewhere, hang on." I grab my purse and then my tote bag, rummaging around until I find the beat-up spiral notebook.

"Are you serious?" Penn looks at me, I can't tell if she is in shock or disgusted at my note taking.

"What? I write everything down."

"But what about the details?"

"The details are so far...," I opened my notebook and turned to the page dated this past weekend. "We are having mini crab cakes, mini shrimp kabobs, hot chicken dip, and a veggie tray for starters." I looked up.

"This is it?"

"Oh no, we, or rather Chuck, have come up with a ton of ideas. I have sampled more food than a normal person should eat in a month. But there is more." I try to reassure her.

"Why haven't you come up with more?"

"Because Chuck wanted a full-blown three-course meal and people want to dance, drink and have a good time. I'm sure Eryn and Blue don't want to sit there all day having a boring lunch when they are excited about their honeymoon. So, I suggested he try a lighter menu that won't take a long time to prepare, serve or eat."

Penn smiled. "Good point."

I sighed, "I guess, it took quite a lot of convincing."

"What's the problem?"

"Chuck," An image of Chuck in a white t-shirt clinging to his muscular chest from the heat of the kitchen, feeding me his latest creation, popped into my head. I pushed it aside. "He is very creative in the kitchen and apparently has all kinds of ideas. He insists on my sampling everything so I can make an informed decision."

Penn laughed, "So what's wrong with having a man cook for you?"

"In theory, nothing."

"Is he good-looking?"

"Well, yeah." I smiled to myself, thinking of Chuck's chiseled good looks. Warm brown eyes that said there was way more to Chuck than those muscular arms, brown curly hair, and a smile that could charm a woman out of her clothes in a hot minute. Although I am working hard to make myself immune to men, there is just something demoralizing about having a good-looking guy sit there and watch you eat your way into a larger dress size.

"So, you are unhappy with the fact that he wants to go all out for his friend's wedding? And second, he is hot and likes to cook for you?"

"When you put it that way, it makes me sound like some sort of...." I wasn't sure of the exact word that would apply here.

"The word is brat."

"Brat? How am I being a brat?"

"Let me explain…"

I held up my hand, cutting Penn off; I wasn't in the mood to listen to what could certainly be a brutally honest assessment of my attitude towards Chuck, and men in general.

"I want Eryn's wedding to be special, and something Eryn would want."

Penn nodded in agreement. "It is a tough balance."

"Not for you, apparently." I point to the book. "You two have been friends for years, so I'm sure you two have discussed your future wedding days and you are confident in what she wants. I haven't known you and Eryn that long, so I am more or less winging it."

"You're doing great, but pictures of the food would be nice."

I laughed, "Okay, next week I will take pictures."

"Great," Penn stood up, "this calls for more ramen."

"I can't eat anything else. I'm gaining weight every time I go to Chuck's."

"So, start coming to the gym with me."

"You work out at the gym?" I'm not sure why this surprised me.

Penn laughed, "I appreciate you consider all of this is natural." She wiggled her slender hips, "but, I work hard to keep this body."

I nod in agreement. "I might have to do that."

"I'll give you the number to my personal trainer and she can get you all set up."

"Thanks." With a plan in place to ward off the extra pounds, I help myself to more ramen.

Chapter 2
Chuck

"It's getting late man; shouldn't you be going home to your fiancé?" I glance at Blue as I wipe down the bar.

Blue shrugged, "Why? She is probably working late again. I swear ever since we set the wedding date she is like a machine. She works all the time trying to get things ready for her to leave the store in someone else's hands for two weeks."

"Have you tried calling her?"

"You're a chef, not a bartender. Why aren't you in the kitchen doing something cheffy?"

"Because the kitchen is closed, and I like to take care of the most troublesome customers myself."

"Hmpf."

"What? Did you expect just because you are the chief of police that you get special treatment?"

"No, I figured it was because I saved your ass more than once in that damn desert."

"That isn't how I remember it." I chuckle.

"I'm sure; I've heard head injuries have caused memory lapses." Blue laughed as he stood up and put money down on the bar.

"How many times do I have to tell you, your money is no good here?"

"It's not for you, it's for him." Blue nodded to Brandon, the bartender on duty who was trying discreetly to clean up the bar so he could go home.

"Oh well, in that case." I took the money and called over my shoulder as I turned towards Brandon, "I'll see ya later."

"See ya." Blue waved.

"Here's a tip from Chief Keegan. You take special care of him whenever he is here, okay?"

Brandon nodded and pocketed the cash.

I turned back to watch Blue as he took his cell phone out of his pocket. Jeremy "Blue" Keegan is the toughest son of a bitch I know. We served in the Marine Corps together and we have fought the enemy and survived, mostly because Blue is too tough to die. He is also as loyal as they come. Our unit got involved in some nasty stuff more than once and Blue never let his men go it alone and he never left a man behind. He carried me to safety when I took shrapnel from a bomb in an ambush attack. He is completely besotted with Eryn Upton. I'm happy for them both, although I don't know Eryn that well, but I have seen the way she looks at Blue, and I believe they are meant to be together. I long for someone to gaze at me the way Eryn looks at Blue. But that would mean I'd have to let someone in, and I've got too much baggage for that. But it doesn't stop my mind from conjuring images of Sarah. She has an intensity about her that is both intimidating and sexy. Sarah is a woman who knows what she wants and how to get it. She is also infuriating as hell sometimes because she will not back down. Sarah was all business with her notebook, pens, and highlighter. She had very specific ideas, and while wedding receptions weren't something I had ever hosted here at the Seabreeze, I had plenty of experience with them when I was still in culinary school, working part time. I realized Sarah had done plenty of research and that we could set up the menu quickly. But that would mean the menu and seating arrangements would be settled; in all likelihood, I would not see her again until the wedding, which was only a month away. I couldn't allow that to happen, and I had to find a way to see more of Sarah, to get to know her despite it being against my better judgment. I was happy to take a woman to dinner, a movie, a festival, but nothing that was too intimate and nothing that was going to lead to anything long-term. Too many of my friends had married and were divorced. Some of them amicable and some of them fiercer than any war I'd ever served in, and I knew that was something I never wanted to live through. But Sarah. Sarah was different. Sarah was worth the risk. So, I devised a plan to try to see her at least once a week.

I had been stringing Sarah along for a while now, finding reasons to meet with her about the reception. I had held my ground over the argument of a formal plated lunch versus lighter fare for the reception as long as I could. Frankly, I agreed with Sarah. She made an excellent point that a formal lunch reception wasn't Blue's style, and I was getting the impression it wasn't Eryn's style either. Now, I was dragging my feet on the finger foods, but I was afraid she was going to see through my charade soon and I needed a new plan to keep Sarah engaged.

The next morning, I went to the restaurant early. I was getting the urge to try something new on the menu. Around ten o'clock Brenda, my front-end manager, arrived.

"Morning Chuck."

"Morning Brenda," I looked up from the recipe I was working on. "Brenda, I have a question for you."

Brenda stopped and leaned against the doorway of my office, "Sure."

"What are your thoughts on expanding the restaurant into hosting more private events or even catering?"

"Whoa, are you serious?"

"I might be. Why?"

"Boss, that is a lot of work and hosting private parties can get really stressful as some of those people are really picky."

I nodded. "I hear ya. You have some experience in this area, don't you?"

"Yes, I do, and that is one reason I work here, so I don't have to deal with that. I'm short-staffed as it is and to get people to work the long hours or weekends can be difficult sometimes."

"So, we would definitely need more staff."

"Yes, and you need a catering manager or someone to run the business side of that. You don't have time unless you are planning on coming out of the kitchen."

Brenda had a good point, and it gave me an idea. I knew it would probably lead to trouble, and I would regret it. I could hire Sarah to be the business manager. It wouldn't solve the problem of more staff or a catering manager, but it would allow me to see more of her. And while I knew it solved one problem, it only created another. While I could see Sarah more often, was it a good idea to date someone in the workplace? Definitely not.

Chapter 3
Sarah

Spring hadn't officially sprung, but the chance of sleet, rain, and high winds wasn't enough to keep things quiet at the garden center. Eryn and I were in the retail store discussing new inventory for spring. I was pitching my ideas to rearrange the displays based on our sales history and inventory tracking software when Penn came swooping in.

"Are you ladies available for a tasting this afternoon?"

"This afternoon? No!" Eryn said, walking away from Penn.

Penn followed, her heels clicking on the concrete floor as she went. "What do you mean, no?"

I ducked for cover behind a display of birdhouses; Eryn hated it when Penn popped in with last-minute plans.

"You can't refuse to sample your own wedding cakes."

"I mean no." Eryn insisted. "And of course, I can. I can refuse anything I want."

"You're being bullheaded," Penn argued.

"Listen, I am happy to sample whatever. But what was wrong with the cakes I tasted last week?"

"Nothing if you're happy with lemon cake and vanilla icing."

"I am, and if you want me to taste any more cakes or try on any dresses, you are going to have to schedule an appointment, just like any other wedding planner. I cannot drop everything to run off in the middle of the day to sample something or pick out napkin designs." Eryn threw her hands in the air in frustration. "Which reminds me, who is running your store while you are here?"

Penn looked as if it hurt her feelings for a moment before regrouping. "Bridgette is minding the store at the moment."

"I thought we settled the cakes or cupcakes or whatever you have planned. Is there a problem with what I picked out last week?"

"Well, no."

"Then I'm not interested in tasting anything else." Eryn looked around and spotted me peering around a display I pretended to be dusting. "That goes for you too. I trust whatever you and Chuck decide on for the reception menu."

"You got it," I called out, choosing to remain out of the fray that was Penn and Eryn.

Eryn turned back to Penn. "See how easy that is?"

Penn pursed her lips, turned on her heel, and left in a huff.

Eryn stood with her hands on her hips "You can come out now."

"You sure?"

"Yes." she looked around as if she was trying to remember what she had been doing before Penn came in. "I'm sorry, but I didn't know getting married could be so stressful. I am halfway tempted to elope."

I gasped.

Eryn held up her hands and shook her head. "don't worry, I won't, but it is tempting."

I watched Penn's Mercedes pull out of the parking lot. "She just wants everything to be perfect." I said, feeling sorry for Penn. The problem was that Penn was going overboard, which was typical. Still, I was surprised by Eryn's reaction, as she should know that is how Penn is by now. Heck, I knew it, and I hadn't been friends with her nearly as long as Eryn.

"I know, I know." Eryn started rearranging some bars of milk soap. "I'll call her later and make it up to her. Let's take a break."

Eryn headed to her office, the soap forgotten.

I followed. "Do you not want to see what Chuck and I decided on, really?"

"You know what I like and don't like. I trust you. Honestly, I'm going to be so excited that day that I will not be focused on the food, no offense."

"None taken." I giggled; I was pleased with myself that I had told both Chuck and Penn the same thing already. "But you seem a bit overwhelmed." I wanted to avoid an outburst like the one with Penn.

Eryn stopped me. "You're right." Eryn sank into her worn office chair.

"I am?"

"Yes, I need to hire more staff, but I just can't handle another thing on my plate right now, so you're going to do it."

"Me?"

"Yes, you, Rick, and Steve."

"I don't understand."

"Talk to them and find out when they are available and then set up a staff meeting."

"Uh, okay." I left in search of Rick and Steve.

Later that afternoon, Rick, Steve, and I squeezed into Eryn's office. Eryn looked up from her computer. "It has been brought to my attention that we might need some more help around here, and as you know I am going to be gone for a couple of weeks next month."

We all nodded.

"This is a perfect time to make some changes. Rick and Steve, you manage your sections of the business very well and from now on you will hire and train any additional help you need."

Rick and Steve looked at each other in surprise. Rick grinned.

"That being said, we have to run it by Sarah for budget purposes and I want to be kept in the loop, but you guys are more than capable of handling it."

"Yes, ma'am." Rick was clearly more excited than Steve.

"And Sarah, you will do the same for the retail area." Eryn smiled.

"What?" I said, not having expected this at all.

"Yes, you understand how that part of the business works as well as I do, and you can handle that with no problem."

I looked at her stunned, "Yeah, sure. I mean, yes, of course."

"Good, now that is settled, I will not be working late tonight, and I will see you all tomorrow."

The three of us looked at each other for a moment, then filed out of Eryn's office.

I left shortly after Eryn. Tuesdays in March weren't particularly busy at the restaurant, so Chuck and I agreed it would be a good time to get together to discuss the menu items. Actually, we met twice a week on Tuesdays and Saturdays, so that I could sample anything that changed from the previous meeting. Penn's words replayed themselves in my head that Chuck wanted to help make Eryn and Blue's wedding just as special as Penn and I did. I was embarrassed for not considering that before. Tonight, I promised myself to have a more open mind about his suggestions.

When I got to the Seabreeze, I was expecting Chuck would have several options for us to discuss. I headed straight back to the bar.

"Hey Sarah, good to see you." Chuck waved me over and led the way to the empty dining room in the back with a beautiful view of the water. "Would you like something to drink before we get started tonight?"

"Yes, thank you."

Chuck was back in a few minutes with a pitcher of iced tea.

"Based on our last conversation, I believe I have the menu completely worked out and I thought we'd go over it tonight."

I sipped my drink, "Sounds good, also, Eryn has decided that the cake is going to be lemon with a vanilla frosting."

"No problem. I'll have some light drinks and punch to complement the cake." Chuck paused for a moment. Before we discuss the menu, I'd like to talk to you about something else.

I nodded for him to continue.

"Since the word has gotten out about the police chief's wedding reception being held here, I've been getting a lot more inquiries. I'm considering expanding my business to include catering events and maybe adding a food truck for off-site events. From a business perspective, what are your thoughts?"

"It sounds like a good idea, but I have no experience in the food industry, so it is not something I am familiar with enough to offer an opinion."

"You may not have experience in this business, but you have a good head for numbers."

Heat stung my cheeks at the compliment.

Chuck pressed on, "You didn't really have any experience with the nursery and landscaping business before you met Eryn, but you seem to do well there."

"That is true, I have learned a lot from Eryn."

"You could learn the business side of the food industry just as quickly if you wanted to, I'm sure." He leaned back in his chair.

I sat wondering if I had heard Chuck correctly. Was he offering me a job? Was he trying to steal me away from Eryn?

"I suppose if I had a reason to, I could," not wanting to dismiss an opportunity out of hand but being careful not to seem eager to abandon Eryn.

"What if I offered you a reason to learn it?"

I shrugged. "I don't know."

Chuck leaned in, his brown eyes drawing me in conspiratorially. "Sarah, come work with me. Be my business manager and help me expand my business. I can't do it alone. I'm a chef and I'm not good with the numbers, not like you."

"I can't leave Eryn now." I shook my head, "not when she is getting ready to go on her honeymoon and everything. She would lose her mind."

"Okay, I understand, but can you help me part-time?"

The prospect of doing something different excited me. I wanted to do more than just work at the garden center, but I felt a loyalty to Eryn. "Can I think about it?"

"Of course." Chuck's charming smile almost made me forget I had sworn off men.

What would it be like working for a man that turned every head in the room and made you think very naughty thoughts? I gave myself a mental headshake, and I refocused on the business at hand.

"So, what's the final menu for the reception?"

Chuck opened a folder and took out a sheet of paper. "Prepare to be impressed."

I studied the menu carefully. He had a good mix of vegetarian-friendly options and seafood and chicken. There were even southern sausage bites.

"This all looks great, Chuck. Thank you."

"Should we invite Eryn and Blue in for samples?"

"No, Eryn made it clear she was tired of sampling and approving every little thing. She and Blue are threatening to elope if we don't give them some space."

Chuck laughed, "I'm sure it wouldn't take much to encourage Blue to elope and get him out of all of this."

I laughed with him, "sounds like they are really perfect for each other."

"Do you want to discuss seating arrangements?" Chuck asked.

"Sure, if we need to. I mean, the standard rectangular table at the front of the room for the wedding party and then smaller either round or square tables for the guests should work." Honestly, I hadn't considered the seating arrangement.

"We could do that, but do you think Eryn and Blue really want to sit up there like royalty looking out over the crowd?" Chuck asked, taking out a clean piece of paper and a pencil ready to make notes.

"I guess you have a point. Did you have anything in mind?" I admonished myself for not thinking of it and grateful Chuck had before Penn realized I had forgotten that detail.

Chuck grinned and began sketching. "What if we place a large round table for the wedding party and then a smaller round table just for Blue and Eryn upfront but slightly off-center so they aren't on display."

"Hmmmm," I took the paper and studied it. "I believe you're on the right track with this."

"Buuuut...," Chuck knew I was about to add something to the design, just like I had done previously with the menu.

"But I'm not sure I like them at a table alone. If the crowd gets distracted, it could be too easy for them to duck out unnoticed."

"I like the way your mind works; I'm relieved that you use your devious powers for good and not evil."

I had to laugh.

"Okay, I'll keep at it." He took the paper back. "I've kept you here longer than I planned. Can I at least offer you dinner?"

"Oh no, that's unnecessary."

"Sure, it is. Unless, of course, you have other plans." He was a smooth talker, and I was sure women usually fell for it every time.

"No, I don't have any plans other than to go home and binge watch TV and probably eat a microwave dinner."

"Oh god!" He held his hand over his heart. "Never tell a chef you are going to eat a frozen microwave meal!"

"Don't you ever just tire of cooking and toss something in the microwave?"

"I would rather toss myself off the James River bridge!" He feigned mortal injury. "At least let me give you something decent to reheat once you get home. I can't bear the image of you eating a frozen heap of preservatives."

"Well, since you put it that way."

"Thank you."

He returned a short time later, carrying a bag.

"Here you go, ma'am."

"Thank you. How much do I owe you?"

"Please," He held his hand up, "just knowing you will have a decent meal tonight is payment enough. And if you like it, tell your friends." He smiled.

"Well, thank you very much. If you keep giving away free food, you are definitely going to need a business manager."

Chuck walked with me to the door. "Please consider my offer, about working with me."

"I will and thank you for the dinner."

I considered his offer on the drive home. I had to admit it was a tempting offer. But the timing was all wrong. I couldn't leave Eryn now, especially since Eryn had entrusted me with more responsibility.

When I got home, I dropped the bag of food, keys, and purse on the counter and headed straight to the bedroom to change clothes. I was exhausted and grateful that I didn't have to attempt any sort of cooking tonight, even in the microwave.

When I opened the bag, there was a note on top.

"If you need to reheat this, please do it in the oven on 350F for six minutes. DO NOT PUT THIS IN THE MICROWAVE. Bon appétit- Chuck,"

A phone number was scrawled under his name. Smiling, I unpacked three boxes, one in a special little insulated bag. I opened that first. A piece of cheesecake with sauce and a strawberry on top greeted me. Oh, Chuck was good, he was very good. I popped the cheesecake into the fridge for later. Then I opened the other two boxes, the first, roasted vegetables with a little plastic cup of freshly grated parmesan cheese. And last, the third container where the aroma of seafood casserole was heavenly. I followed the reheating instructions and put everything on a plate and headed to the sofa. A romance movie was just starting as I took a bite of the casserole. I savored the flavor. It practically melted in my mouth. I wondered if it was because it has been ages since I'd eaten food prepared from scratch or was Chuck that good.

With my meal complete, I decided the cheesecake could wait until later. It would be my special treat with a glass of wine. I retrieved the note from the kitchen table and tapped the numbers into my phone and typed out a text message.

"Thank you again. The dinner was amazing. Do you have a wine recommendation for the cheesecake?"

Hesitating, I pondered what Penn would do in this situation and then pressed the send button. I shoved the phone in the pocket of my sweatpants and returned to the sofa to finish the movie. My phone buzzed almost right away.

"I recommend a raspberry or cheery beer. Either of those is probably a better match for strawberry cheesecake than wine."

"I've never had either of those," I replied, giggling.

"Or, I have a wonderful Cabernet Franc I could bring over, plus the rest of the cheesecake."

I blushed, even though Chuck couldn't see me.

"And let you see me in my sweatpants, no way!"

"Sweatpants are the preferred attire for cheesecake." He added a laughing emoji.

"I'll stick with the white wine I have in the fridge."

"Have you learned nothing during our brief time together?"

"I guess I'm a slow learner."

"Not at all, let me know if you want lessons."

I studied the phone for a long moment before I sent my reply. "I will."

Nestling back down into the sofa, pulling an afghan up. I imagined what it might be like to sip wine in the candlelight with Chuck. Then, pushed the thought from my mind. My track record with men wasn't something to fool around with, I felt like Chuck was a great guy. The problem was, I was normally attracted to jerks and psychopaths. So, it was probably best to keep my distance.

Chapter 4
Chuck

Business was picking up in the restaurant; the weather was sporadically warm this week, and people were hoping for an early spring. I was at the hostess stand checking on the seating when Blue and Eryn came in.

"Hey, Chief. Eryn, it's good to see you again."

"Hi Chuck, I hope you don't mind I tagged along for Blue's weekly visit."

"Are you kidding? I wish he brought you with him more often. I'm tired of talking to him all the time."

"This place is packed tonight." Blue looked around.

"The bar is full; would you like a table in the back?"

"If it isn't too much trouble." Eryn gave me a smile that exposed her dimples.

"No trouble. I'll join you in a bit," I had a hostess show Blue and Eryn to a quiet table.

According to Sarah, Eryn didn't want to sample anything, I couldn't resist taking something out to the table.

"I have something I need you to try for me."

"Chuck, man, we've had dinner. We just stopped in for a drink and to say hello."

"No problem, this won't fill you up at all, just a bite." I sat a small plate in front of each of them. "Go on."

"Better try it. He won't go away until we do," Blue advised.

Eryn took a bite. "Hmm, what is that? Some sort of pastry with honey?"

"Yes, very good. I'm trying out a few new recipes."

Blue eyed me suspiciously. "Tastes pretty good. Better than the chocolate coconut thing you tried the last time."

"Oh yeah, well, I should have known that wouldn't work."

"Yeah." Blue handed me the plate back.

"I can see you are going to be hard to please, I'll be back."

"Chuck, don't come back here without a beer." Blue narrowed his gaze.

"Fine." I returned to the kitchen. I wanted them to try the beer cheesecake combo I had been working on, so I grabbed a couple of raspberry beers and the cheesecake.

"Okay, this will be more to your liking." I presented them both with cheesecake and beer, the same combination I had suggested to Sarah.

Eryn looked down at the two dubiously. "I've never had beer and cheesecake together."

Blue gave me a knowing glance.

"Oh, you'll love this. This is a Belgian style raspberry beer; it goes perfectly with the strawberry cheesecake."

Blue pushed the plate and the beer away. "Hard pass."

Eryn was a good sport. "I'll try it, Chuck."

"Okay, sample the cheesecake, first."

Eryn took a small bite.

"Now a sip of beer," I waited for Eryn to pass judgement.

"That is good."

"Right? You try it, Blue."

"You bring me a beer flavored beer, or I'll have you arrested for offenses against beer."

"You are seriously no fun." I removed his plate and the raspberry beer.

"Uh, Chuck," Eryn held out her hand. You can leave his beer for me. "I see this is going to be a two-beer night."

"That's my girl." Blue laughed.

I returned with a beer for Blue. "Here you go, man. Eryn, please excuse me, I have to go take care of a few things in the kitchen."

"Chuck, if Blue is being an ass, I apologize."

"Eryn, you are so sweet. What you are doing with him, I have no idea. But, no, my kitchen staff has somehow gotten themselves behind on the orders and I need to go fix it." I winked at Eryn. "Oh and let me know if you want that cheesecake at your reception. I'll have to run it past Sarah, of course."

Eryn laughed as I turned away. "I'll let you know." She called out.

Desserts aren't normally my expertise. My forte is more the main courses, savory dishes with passion. But something about Sarah reminded me of sweet desserts and I wanted to create something special. I get creative when I'm in a new relationship, but this was different. Sarah and I weren't in a relationship. I had offered her the job, because I needed a business manager and, I'm sure once the wedding is over, I'll never see her again. Trying something new was exciting. I pulled a wild array of ingredients from the pantry and stared at them, trying to picture something in my mind from the endless possibilities.

Sarah's face kept popping into my brain, interrupting my baking thoughts. "Dammit!" I turned away from the table of ingredients. What was I thinking? This had disaster written all over it and yet I couldn't stop myself. I couldn't stop thinking about Sarah. This was crazy. Where was this coming from? How well did I really know her? We met up twice a week and we only ever talked about the wedding and nothing about her. All I knew was that she worked for and was a good friend to Eryn. I sighed and went back to my table and began moving ingredients around like chess pieces, grouping them together and considering what I could make with them and then rearranging them again. I did this for hours, making notes before putting everything away and going home.

Despite being tired I couldn't sleep instead I grabbed a beer from the fridge and went into the living room and sat down. I turned on the TV, more out of habit than any genuine interest in watching it. I flipped through the channels stopping on an old western. With the volume muted the images as they flashed across the screen. I finished my beer and fell asleep on the couch.

I woke with a start sweating; I had been dreaming of explosions and men laying on the ground around me. An arm was laying just out of reach. I felt icy fear in the pit of my stomach and prayed that it wasn't my arm. Then Sarah was bending over me telling me everything was going to be alright. She didn't belong there, and I bolted awake. I looked around the room, trying to get my bearings. The dream wasn't new, but Sarah's face being a part of it was, and it scared the hell out of me. My hands were shaking, and I got up and starting walking around the house, trying to stop my heart from racing.

Blue and I had an arrangement, what when either of us had these night terrors we called the other for support. I hated to call him now, as he was probably sleeping peacefully next to Eryn. I stepped outside into the night air and took a deep breath, then another. I couldn't get enough. I regained some control and decided maybe a run would help work out the rest of my anxiety. I went inside and changed, and I checked the time, four o'clock. I headed out the door and ran for five miles before my brain settled back down. At the Lions Bridge. I stopped and enjoyed the peace and quiet before taking a slow jog back home.

Chapter 5
Sarah

I woke up early Saturday morning with the TV still on. I rolled off the sofa and my cell phone fell on the floor. The screen lit up; I saw Chuck's text from last night. That was trouble waiting to happen. His job offer kept looping in my head. It was a step up from what I was doing at the garden center with Eryn, Finally, around ten o'clock, I couldn't wait any longer. I reasoned Penn should be ready to face the world, so I sent her a text.

"Do you have time for a chat today?"

"Sure, want to come by the store, or meet up for lunch later?"

"The store is fine."

"I'll be in around eleven," Penn answered.

"Thanks, Penn."

At noon, the door chime alerted anyone in the store I had arrived. "Penn, it's me."

"Oh hi, Sarah. Come on back." Penn called from the doorway leading to the backrooms.

I always marveled at the bolts of material and design sketches Penn had around. The back room was colorful and creative. I loved being here. She was always playing chill music, and the vibe was a different side of Penn that most people never saw.

"What's going on? Everything alright with the reception plans?"

"Oh yeah, the menu is all set, the seating arrangements are just about complete

"Great, well I'm glad your part is going well."

Her tone hinted that her side of things wasn't going as smoothly. "Are you having trouble; do you need some help?"

"Not unless you can do something about Eryn."

I laughed, "I'm afraid not."

"How did you get her to taste all the food?" Penn demanded.

"I didn't."

"What?"

"I didn't ask her. She said she wanted me to handle it and I did. I sampled the food, and I trust Chuck. It isn't like she will focus on the food, anyway. If she even eats. Eryn will be too focused on Blue, and the food is for everyone else."

"You sound like Eryn."

"She is rubbing off on me," I laughed.

Penn narrowed her gaze. "I'm not sure that is a good thing. So, what did you want to talk about today?" She asked, while circling me and sizing me up, the way she did when she wanted me to try on one of her new creations, I did a little modeling for her from time to time. I never would have imagined being tall and gangly would come in so handy as an adult.

"Oh well, something came up related to the reception plans." I paused and took a deep breath. "Chuck offered me a job."

"What?" Penn looked surprised and stopped toying with a red pencil.

"Yeah, he wants to expand the restaurant's banquet options and add a food truck. He said he needs a business manager, and he asked me to do it."

"What did you say?"

"I gave him a soft, no."

"Why?"

"That is what I wanted to talk to you about."

She pegged me with a stare. "Okay, let's have it." She sat on the edge of her desk; arms folded.

I was suddenly self-conscious. "Well," I paced, "first I told him I couldn't quit my job at the garden center now, not with Eryn getting ready to get married and leaving for two weeks."

Penn nodded.

"He asked me to do it part time until after Eryn came back."

"What did you say to that?"

"I told him I'd consider it."

"Are you kidding?"

"Well, I honestly don't know what I want. I mean, I want to further my career, but I'm not sure what that even means for me exactly. Not yet, anyway. I love working with Eryn and she might see it as a betrayal, especially since she just gave me more responsibility."

Penn rolled her eyes. "I get you are still trying to decide what you want your career to be long term but how are you going to figure that out if you are sitting in a tiny office in the garden center?"

I stopped pacing and looked at Penn. "I hadn't thought of it that way," I admitted.

"And Eryn is a big girl. She will understand if you want to do something else. Lord knows she had a ton of jobs before she opened that nursery, which I will never understand that decision."

"You don't agree with her decision to have her own business?"

"No, she should have her own business if that is what she wants. I just do not understand the attraction to the landscape business.

"What else could she have done?"

"She loves the water, and she can't stand not to be near it, so I'm surprised she didn't choose something that involved the water, like a charter boat company, swimming, sailing, scuba lessons, surfing lessons or a surf shop. I mean the list is endless, and she has plenty of experience in all of those things."

I felt the need to defend Eryn as she seems right at home in the garden center, and she really seems to love plants. I hesitated, then asked, "What made you choose fashion design, that seems like a pretty tough business to break into and be successful? You did some of those things that Eryn did too, right?"

"Eryn talks too much." Penn frowned, realizing that Eryn must have included her in our discussion of their younger days, "But, yes,

I was wild and a bohemian once too. We traveled to Europe one summer," Penn sighed, and a faraway expression appeared in her eyes. "And I saw all these glamorous looking women and men and they looked like they had such an exciting life and got to meet beautiful, exciting people. I wanted to be part of that."

"I can understand that, but if you don't mind my asking why do that in Gates Point? I mean, it isn't exactly the fashion capital of the east."

"That is true." She picked up the pencil again and started fidgeting with it. "I like to believe that I bring fashion to the masses, those who might not otherwise have access to fashions from Milan and Paris."

Penn was evading the question. But I would not press her too hard for an answer. She had a quick temper.

"I get it," I nodded.

She refocused on me. "So, what is it you want to do?"

"I haven't decided. I see you and Eryn being successful business owners and I guess I want to be like you, but I'm just not sure how."

"So, you are a trained accountant, but do you see yourself crunching numbers all day, sitting alone at a desk?"

"No, not really."

"What is it you like most about your job right now?"

"I like that Eryn includes me in other parts of the business and I enjoy doing a little of everything talking to customers, helping Eryn, but also doing the budget."

"Then you need to take that job with Chuck. It sounds like it will be more of the parts of the job you love, plus the number crunching. You don't have to work for Chuck the rest of your life. Do it for a while, gain some experience and move on."

"I see your point." I agreed. "Plus, there are other perks to that job."

"Really what is that?"

I smiled a mischievous smile. "Chuck is one hell of a chef."

"Don't forget you are still one of my best models, so don't go ruining that beautiful waistline!"

"You'll just have to make your clothes for curvy girls!"

"I make my clothes for all sizes and shapes!"

"Really?"

"Yes ma'am, all my styles come in every shape and size and if there is something that doesn't quite fit someone, then I will make it for them. That's what makes my shop so special. You can be of any size and get the same beautiful clothes as supermodels."

"I guess I didn't realize that."

"That is because you don't have any curves."

I looked down at myself. "I have one or two."

Penn smiled. "Your beautiful regardless of any curves you have or don't have."

"Thanks!"

Chapter 6

Chuck

I hadn't taken a day off since I opened the Seabreeze two years ago, and I wanted to do some exploring. With the restaurant and bar managers in charge over the weekend, I drove out to Gloucester County in search of a variety of organic honeys and visited several farmers' markets around the Richmond area. I then headed south on Sunday to Emporia, Zuni, and Chesapeake.

I made some new connections for local cheese and honey I found during my local food adventure. Excited about my new finds I went home and started experimenting. I was elbow deep in flour for a new pastry when the doorbell rang Sunday evening.

"Who is it?" I never opened my door without asking the person on the other side to identify themselves.

"Blue."

I opened the door. "Hey man, what are you doing here?"

"I could ask you the same thing; I stopped by the restaurant, and they said you took the weekend off?"

"Yeah, I had the urge to go shopping at some farmers' markets and stuff. Come in the kitchen, I'm in the middle of something."

"Dude, this is getting serious."

I turned to Blue, "What do you mean? I haven't had a day off in two years. What's wrong with taking a break?"

"Because this is what you do every time you date someone new."

"I'm not dating anyone."

"Really?"

"Yeah, really. I just want to try something different."

"And you have met no one new lately?"

"No," I paused, "Well, yeah, I mean I've met new people lately but not romantically."

Blue eyed me suspiciously. "So, who've you met, in a non-romantic way?"

"I don't know, lots of people."

"Name a female out of this group of 'lots of people.'"

"Okay, well let's see." I was stalling. Blue was going to try to trip me up. Sometimes it sucked having a friend whose life's work involved getting people to tell him something they didn't want to tell.

"Oh okay, Sarah, for one. That isn't romantic, she is just planning your wedding reception."

"Sarah?" Blue studied me, looking for signs of deception. "Sarah, that works for Eryn, who is tall, with dark black hair and soft brown eyes?"

Blue was right, those eyes were warm and soft; they reminded me of a long night sitting next to a cozy fire at the beach under the stars.

"Yes, she does have nice hair."

"Bullshit!" Blue shouted, walking to the fridge. "I'm going to drink one of your beers."

"Go ahead." I continued to roll out the pastry dough.

Blue leaned against the kitchen sink behind me.

"So, you've been meeting with Sarah to plan the reception and suddenly you have the urge to create new recipes and there is nothing romantic between you two?"

"That's right."

"She turned you down, didn't she?" Blue chuckled.

I turned to face Blue, "What do you mean?"

"I mean you asked her out, and she said no."

"No, I didn't ask her out." For a moment, I thought Blue had found out that I had offered Sarah a job. Grateful that he focused on the dating theme, I turned back to my pastry and added the butter required to create the light, flaky layers.

"So, you were rejected, but not for a date? What was the question?"

"I hate it when you do this. It is none of your business. Shouldn't you be spending time with Eryn?"

Blue grabbed my arm. "You didn't ask her just to sleep with you, did you?"

"No! What kind of ass do you think I am?"

Relieved, Blue let go. "What's up with you, man? I've known you a long time and I can tell when something is on your mind. And you look like crap, have you been sleeping?"

I thought about the dreams that now included Sarah; there was no way I was going to tell him about that now. "Can I please just finish this and get it in the fridge before I subject myself to your inquisition?"

"Sure, go ahead." Blue raised his hands in mock surrender and took a few steps back.

"Thank you."

I stepped past Blue to the refrigerator, doing my best to avoid eye contact.

"Okay, so you aren't dating Sarah or anyone." Blue continued, "But that doesn't mean you aren't developing feelings for her."

I stopped what I was doing and sighed heavily; I know he would not give up, he was like a bulldog, "Listen, I offered Sarah a job, okay?"

"You what?"

"Yeah, I want to expand, and I need a business manager. I've watched how she had handled me in organizing this reception and she had a good head for business, she isn't a pushover, and she is good with money," I shrugged, "so I asked her to come work for me and help me expand."

"And she said, no?"

"Well, she didn't say yes."

Blue started laughing.

"What is so funny?"

"All this time I believed it was newfound love that made you creative when it is actually the rejection."

"You know what, Blue. You can take your insights, that beer, and...."

"Okay, okay." Blue finished his beer. "What did Sarah say, when you offered her the job?"

"She said she couldn't leave Eryn right now, not before the wedding."

"And you said?"

"I said I totally understood that and why didn't she take some time to think about it. In meantime, she agreed to help me on a part-time basis to get the business plan and paperwork together to finance the expansion."

Blue looked thoughtful.

Suddenly I was worried he would go home and tell Eryn. "You're not going to tell Eryn, are you?"

"Seriously? You think I am going to risk ruining my honeymoon, no way!"

"Okay, thanks."

"I gotta go, I'll talk to you later." He headed for the door and showed himself out.

Taking a break while my pastry chilled and started working on the chocolate sauce. I should have told Blue about the dream, but I didn't want to be hassled anymore about my feelings for Sarah. I should have given him more credit that, but I couldn't bring myself to say the words. I needed to get a hold of myself. I thought the baking would keep my mind off thin, but it was only making them worse. I thought about Sarah tasting the pastries and telling me how good they were in some twisted reception planning fantasy. I really need to clear my head. I finished my work in the kitchen and went for another run. At this rate, I'd qualify for the Marine Corps Marathon.

Chapter 7

Sarah

It was a typical Sunday morning; I woke up with no particular plans for the day. I was drinking my morning coffee when my phone buzzed with a text from Chuck.

"Still willing to help me part time?"

I chewed my lip for a moment. With Penn's words echoing in my mind, I then typed "Yes."

"That's great! When do you want to meet?"

"Shouldn't we set up a schedule?"

"That is an excellent idea. Can I call you?"

"Sure."

A moment later, my phone rang. I took a deep breath. This still felt like a betrayal to me, but I had to look out for my future. I answered the phone.

"Hello."

"Hi, Sarah. Thank you for agreeing to help me. Setting up a work schedule is a great idea."

"Sure, no problem." I heard myself say the words, but my heart knew there was definitely a problem. I was conflicted about putting myself before my friend's needs. There was also the problem that Chuck was so smoking hot that just the sound of his voice made me want to do things that would cause my grandmother to blush. I closed my eyes and pushed the thoughts away.

"I'm gonna have to schedule my hours around my job with Eryn and any last-minute things I need to do to help with the wedding. The problem I foresee is that your free time is probably when I'm working at the garden center."

"That's true, but if we only meet twice a week, I think I can swing that. What do you think about Saturday and Sundays? I don't want to take up your entire weekend, maybe we can do the mornings?"

"Actually, that might work better for me." I felt the excitement flutter in my stomach.

"Great, we can start next weekend here at the restaurant since the place will be closed; we can spread out on one of the tables if we need to."

"Sounds perfect, eight o'clock, too early for you?" I was ready for this new challenge. I was a little disappointed I would have to wait a whole week.

"I'll have the coffee ready." Chuck agreed.

"See you then." We clicked off. I smiled to myself at the prospect of learning something new.

It wasn't long after I hung up with Chuck that the phone buzzed again.

"Hello?"

"Sarah, it's Penn. You want to have lunch today?"

"Sure, where shall I meet you?"

"How about the Grey Goose? I'm in the mood for comfort food." Penn suggested.

"Sounds perfect," I said, looking out the window at the cloudy skies. March wasn't giving up without a fight this year and despite having had a few days with the temperatures in the sixties, the wind had shifted blowing from the north. I grabbed my favorite sweater and forty-five minutes later, Penn and I sat at a corner table with hot tea with the promise of soup and a ham biscuit on the way.

"So, what has you eating carbs today?" I asked, knowing Penn never ate carbs.

"Richard and I broke up."

"Who's Richard?"

"You know, the handsome man who owns the car dealership."

"No." I shook my head. I had no idea who she was talking about.

"Honestly, do you even listen to me when I'm talking?"

"Have I met him?"

"Oh, probably not." Penn waved her hand dismissively.

"Then why do you think I know him?"

"Because you've heard me talk about him."

I remembered Penn talking about going out to dinner a few times, but I didn't recall her ever using the man's name, so I assumed it was a different guy for each date.

"Had you been dating him long?"

"About four months."

I was surprised, four months to Penn was like a year to anyone else as far as relationships were concerned. "Wow, what happened?"

"He said he wants to see other people."

"You guys were exclusive?"

Penn sighed. "Apparently he thought so."

The food came, and the conversation lulled.

Rejuvenated, Penn took a deep breath. "Don't let men hold you back, Sarah, you don't need them."

"Okay," I agreed, not that I had any suitors to hold me back, and I certainly didn't want any. Rob had been the last straw in the dating world for me. When you go out with a guy and he decides you will marry, have kids, and he will control your life, after only three dates you know it's time to move on.

Penn quickly changed the subject, "I hope you told that guy Chuck, no."

"No, why would I do that? You said I should try different things."

"That was before Richard broke my heart."

Sighing I sensed a melodramatic moment coming on. Penn would mourn the loss of this relationship until someone new came along. It was always that way. She would walk around being melodramatic until another man caught her eye and then Richard would be forgotten.

"I already told him I would help him part time on the weekends. Because that is all I have time for."

"Points to you for not letting him dictate the schedule."

"The thing is that now that we have set up a schedule and everything. I find myself really excited about it."

"Excited in what way?"

"Well, I am eager to learn about the food industry and what goes on behind the scenes."

"Are you sure that is all you're excited about?"

"Yes, of course."

Monday came too soon. I found I wasn't as excited about work today as I normally am. I was already wracked with guilt about working part time for Chuck, and I was dreading having to tell Eryn.

It was sunny and a little chilly this morning; the weather continued to be sporadic as one minute it felt like spring and the next the winds would shift; the clouds were rolling in reminding me that winter wasn't over yet. Eryn's car was already in the parking lot, which wasn't surprising. She was routinely the first one in and the last one to leave. But lately, she had been doing better about spending more time at home with Blue and less time after normal business hours.

I had a moment of déjà vu as I opened the door. I flashed back to a year ago when Rob, aka stalker ex-boyfriend, had broken into the garden center after hours and kidnapped Eryn to get my attention. For some reason, he thought I would see what a great guy he was if he kidnapped my boss.

I shook off the memories and found Eryn in the kitchenette, waiting impatiently for the coffee to brew.

"Good morning, Eryn." I tried to sound like a happy morning person, which I wasn't.

"Oh, good morning. Isn't it a beautiful day? Looks like we are going to get an early spring."

I frowned. "You really think so?"

"Well, the lows are only going to be in the forties for the next ten days and we only have a couple of weeks until April."

"I would expect you to be a little more cautious about the potential for frost."

"When did you become such a gloomy, Gus? The sun is shining, and we are expecting an order of seeds and onion sets in today." She said, smiling as the coffee made its gurgling noise that indicated it was finished brewing.

I sat my bag down on the table and sank into a chair while Eryn happily poured two cups of coffee. "Can I talk to you for a minute?"

Eryn, sensing my angst, slowly sat down across from me. "Sure, what's wrong?"

"I have to tell you something, and I hope you're not going to be upset with me. I mean, it seemed like a good idea, but now I'm not so sure. Now I feel guilty and," I sighed, "and I'm having some serious doubts about it all."

"Slow down. Why don't you start by telling me what in the world you are talking about?"

I closed my eyes and took a deep breath. "I told Chuck I would help him part time on the weekends to draw up a business plan so he can expand the restaurant. "

"Okay...."

I exhaled, not realizing I had been holding my breath while waiting for her to respond. I tried to gauge her reception of the news.

"Sarah, is that it?"

"Yeah, that's it."

"I'm not sure I understand. Why were you so stressed about telling me you are helping Chuck? He's a great guy and I'm sure he will be very grateful for your expertise."

"It's just on the weekends and...."

Eryn held up her hand. "Sarah, it's okay. Did you think I would get mad?"

"Well, yes, no. I wasn't sure. I feel like I am cheating on you or something."

Eryn laughed. "Sarah, I don't mind if you work part time, volunteer, or whatever. As your employer and your friend, I want you to do whatever makes you happy."

"I guess I sound like a babbling idiot."

"No, you're not an idiot, a little hilarious, maybe." She laughed again and took my hand. "You do what makes you happy. Never worry about what other people think, not me and certainly not Penn."

I laughed. "Okay, promise." I nodded.

"Great. Plus, Chuck isn't bad looking." She winked at me.

"Oh, no! No thank you, I'm done with dating."

"You can't let one psycho stalker ex-boyfriend prevent you from dating."

"Seriously, Eryn, he was nuts, and he kidnapped you!"

"True, but there was a silver lining."

"You can't be serious?" I put my hands on my hip, trying to imagine what would possibly be the silver lining in that nightmare.

"I am serious." She nodded. "Blue rescued me and the rest is history."

I shook my head. "You and Blue were already on the path to a long-term relationship. I don't believe getting kidnapped is what attracted you to Blue."

Eryn nudged my cup of coffee closer to me. "Here, drink this, you'll feel better."

"I'm fine."

"Hmmm, hmmm, I'm going to go put some inventory away."

"Need any help?"

"No, I got it. You just drink your coffee and try to get a hold of yourself." She laughed and left me alone in the kitchenette.

Chapter 8
Sarah

The week was dragging, and I found I was eager for the weekend and for my first lesson in the food industry. I got through the interviews for the position in the retail department with a little less enthusiasm than I should. When Saturday finally arrived, I was awake before the alarm went off. I jumped out of bed. showered, and then came the terrifying realization that I had given little thought to what I should wear. I stood staring blankly into my closet, trying to decide. It was a business meeting, so I didn't want to dress too casually. The weather wasn't cold, but it was chillier than it had been earlier in the week. I needed something with long sleeves. Finally, I decided on a pair of wool slacks, an Oxford shirt with a cardigan, and comfortable shoes. I made tea and toast for breakfast, but even that was too much, I was too excited to finish it.

When I arrived, there was a motorcycle in the parking lot, and I assumed it was Chuck's. Funny, I never pictured him as someone who was into motorcycles. The door was open, and I stepped inside, but then wasn't sure where I should go from there. I was used to coming here when there were people around.

"Hello, Chuck?" No response, so I headed towards the bar. I walked closer to the kitchen area, so I called out again.

"Hello?"

Unsure of where to go next, I stood there for a minute, looking around. I wondered if the motorcycle was in fact Chuck's but rather one of his employees and what would they do if they found me standing there in the middle of the bar when they weren't even open yet. I turned and started to head back to the front.

"Hey, Sarah." Chuck appeared from the kitchen, "I'm sorry I didn't hear you come in."

I blushed. "I'm probably a little early,"

"I was going to make some coffee back here, you interested?" He stepped behind the bar and started working the coffee maker. "We could work out here, my office is tiny and frankly a mess."

"This is fine." I slid onto a barstool.

"Great, so where should we start?" He asked.

"Well, first of all, I know absolutely nothing about the restaurant business or the food industry at all, so maybe you can start by giving me a little background on how things work; like how often you get deliveries and for what kinds of items. When is your busiest time of day, week, or year?"

"Okay, well that is easy enough."

We sat for hours while Chuck explained the basics of the business. He added the extra details specific to the bar when describing the supplies, training the staff, the different hours of operation, and the various regulations. We drank the entire pot of coffee, and I wasn't sure if it was the caffeine or the act of learning something new, but I was excited. "Wow, that is a lot to take in."

"Yeah, it is, and you won't remember it all, so don't worry about it. It takes years to get the hang of the whole thing."

"And you've been doing this by yourself?"

"Well, not entirely. I have a bar manager, a Sous Chef and a waitstaff supervisor.

I had a new appreciation for Chuck. "Still, that is an awful lot to do alone, plus you create new dishes and handle special events like the wedding reception."

Chuck smiled and rubbed his chin. "The wedding reception is a special case; I'm handling that personally because of Blue."

"I almost forgot you guys know each other from the service, right?"

"That's right." Chuck rolled up his shirtsleeves as he poured us each a glass of water, and I noticed the tattoos on his arms. I wondered how far up they went, and I was fascinated by them.

Chuck caught me staring. "Do they bother you?"

The heat rose in my cheeks at being caught. "No, not at all. I was admiring them."

"Thank you, some people are into tattoos, some aren't."

"I'm not sure any of my friends have them and if they do, they are in places I've never seen." I giggled a little.

"I bet a few of them have tats and you just don't know it."

I suddenly wondered if Penn had a tattoo. She and Eryn had been wild in their youth. It wouldn't surprise me if they did, although I imagined Penn would probably have had hers removed or something. "Did you get all of those when you were in the military?"

"No, many of them I got after."

"Were you a cook back then, and is that how you got into the restaurant business?"

Chuck regarded me for a moment. I was starting to get the impression he wasn't going to answer the question and wondered if I had gone too far. "I'm sorry that was a very personal question."

"No, not really." Chuck shook his head.

"You don't have to tell me." I shifted in my seat, uncomfortably.

"Sarah, it's alright." Chuck leaned on the bar and covered my fidgeting hands with his. "Cooking was something that was a hobby until after I got out of the military. Then I worked in a couple of restaurants and fell in love with it. So, I used my GI Bill to go to culinary arts school and here I am."

"That is awesome." I tried to remain neutral and didn't ask any follow-up questions. I had the distinct impression despite Chuck's reassurances that something about that question had hit a nerve, and I didn't want to ruin what had been a wonderful morning by pressing too hard. Some of the kitchen staff had arrived to prepare for the lunch crowd.

"I guess I'd better be going," I said, hoping Chuck didn't hear the disappointment in my voice.

He looked over his shoulder at the employees milling about, getting things ready. "I guess I probably need to get back to the kitchen. See you tomorrow?"

"Yes, see ya. Eight o'clock, okay?" I asked, trying to hide the fact that I really didn't want to leave. I wanted to stay and watch how things worked.

"Sounds perfect. Tomorrow wear jeans though. I am going to let you hang out in the kitchen while we get brunch going and I don't want you to get your clothes ruined."

I smiled at the idea. "Okay, that sounds exciting."

It was mid-morning, and I had the rest of the day ahead of me. I didn't like the idea of going home to sit in my apartment. I needed something to do. I needed to burn off this energy.

Normally I help at the garden center on Saturdays, even though working weekends was not a requirement. Today I wasn't in the mood. I wanted to do something different. Going to Penn's boutique was out of the question. That would only lead to an interrogation from Penn about the meeting with Chuck. So, I drove around the city trying to decide what to do. I spotted the library when I had an idea. I whipped into the parking lot and rushed inside.

A woman about my age was standing at a desk beneath a sign that read 'Information'. "Can I help you?"

"Where would I start if I wanted to learn more about the food industry?"

"We have some wonderful books over there about the culinary arts and then over in the business section we might find you something." The librarian led the way to the stacks.

"Let's start with the business section," I suggested.

The librarian helped me find a couple of books, "The community college also offers some food industry related classes in the continuing education department. They are geared more towards starting a catering business, but they might interest you."

"Yes, thank you." I checked out the books and took them home. Suddenly I had the urge to learn everything there was to learn about running a restaurant. It was important for me to understand what Chuck was talking about when we met tomorrow. I spent the rest of the day reading and taking notes. Finally, when I couldn't read anymore, I turned on the TV and started watching cooking shows. I hoped it would help prepare me at least a little for what I might see in the kitchen tomorrow.

Sunday was a whirlwind. Chuck sat me at a table in the rear of the kitchen, out of the way so that I could observe firsthand what goes on.

The best way to describe it from my perspective was chaos, sheer chaos. I'm sure it must have all made sense to Chuck and his team. But to a layperson, I could barely keep up with what was happening.

The waitstaff entered food orders from computer stations in what Chuck called the front of the house. There was a monitor above the prep area in the kitchen where a person was assigned to call out the orders. Usually, it was Chuck unless he had to step away. He was barking out the names of dishes and times. In some ways, it was like what I had watched on TV the night before only intensified. Tempers flared at times, food and plates were dropped and sometimes an entire order would have to be remade. Each time that happened, the restaurant lost money. If a customer was forced to wait longer than expected for their meal, Chuck might offer them a free dessert or drink, which cost even more money. I knew there was an acceptable amount of loss built into the equation, but still, it was a loss. It was inventory wasted and time lost in preparing the same meal over again. Which meant the table was occupied longer and less money made freeing up the seat for the next paying customer. It was enough to make your head spin. Then there were the deliveries that were late, supply orders that were short or just wrong, causing the menu to be changed for the day to accommodate the situation.

Chuck was good at thinking on his feet. He didn't fluster easily, only when avoidable mistakes were made. But even then, he didn't yell at his employees; it seemed just knowing that they had disappointed him was its own punishment. Some took it harder than others. I was glad I had taken his advice and wore jeans; by the end of the day, I had just as much food on me as the staff. I was rewarded with a wonderful meal after the evening service had slowed down enough for the staff to take a break from prepping and cooking to cleaning and grabbing a quick bite of their own.

Chuck sat with me. "So, what did you think?"

"That was intense," I said, shaking my head. "I don't know how you do it every day."

"It is a rush, I love it." He smiled.

"It seemed pretty hectic."

"Oh, it is. It's completely crazy, but it all works, and food gets out the door and that is the important thing," he admitted.

"And you don't find that stressful at all?"

"Sometimes, sure, we all do. We want the food to be perfect, the guest experience to be perfect and even though we try our best we don't always do our best, and that is frustrating. The food on the plate is an art, and it needs to reflect who we are. When it doesn't well, it can be hard sometimes."

"I can see that. But this," I pointed to the filet mignon in front of me. "Is definitely perfection."

Chuck laughed. "Good, I'm glad you like it. So now that you have seen how things work a little around here, do you want to tackle the numbers?"

"I thought you'd never ask." I smiled.

"I can give you the files so you can review them at your convenience this week and then call me when you're done, and we can set up a time to go over things together if you like."

I finished my dinner and sipped the red wine. "I would like that very much."

Chuck gave me a boyish grin.

As he was walking me to the door, one of the waitstaff rushed over.

"You're not leaving, are you?" She said, batting her eyes in his direction.

"No, I'm not leaving," he answered her, giving her a sweet smile.

"Oh okay, remember you promised me a ride on that big bike of yours after work."

"I didn't forget."

The girl glanced at me as if noticing me for the first time and gave me a wicked smile as she tossed her blonde wavy hair and sauntered off.

I blinked in her direction. Had that just happened? Why did this girl think I cared if she and Chuck were going riding after work?

I turned to face Chuck and reached out to shake his hand, "I'll review the files and get back to you."

"Thanks, Sarah."

Chapter 9
Chuck

I gave Brittany a ride home after work, as promised. She lived all the way on the east side of town in a garden apartment. Traffic could make it a long commute to work, and her old car had finally died. She had been carpooling with the other employees all week, and I had promised to help her out if she got stuck without a ride.

"You want to come in for a while?" Brittany asked, stepping off the back of my bike.

"No, I have somewhere I need to be. "Another time?"

Brittany didn't hide her disappointment, and I'm not sure why I turned her down. She was funny, attractive; had her act together, mostly; she wasn't flighty. Normally, I would take advantage of those qualities. But not today. I really didn't have anywhere I needed to be, but, found myself thinking of Sarah. I shook my head. I didn't need that sort of complication in my life, especially not now that I was trying to expand the restaurant. But every day I seemed to think of Sarah more and more. By the time the weekends arrived, I was aching to see her. I kept telling myself that Sarah was a serious girl I did not need a serious relationship. No commitments were the name of the game; I had held true to that motto for many years. But now, it was getting harder and harder to remember those words when I was around Sarah.

I rode my bike out to the beach. The salt air and the breeze off the water were exactly what I needed to clear my head and refocus. I loved how the sound of the waves pushed everything else out of my head for a while. I could close my eyes and just relax with the smell of the salt air as the cure to my overworked brain.

It was Thursday evening when Sarah finally called.

"Hi Chuck, are you busy?"

"Dinner service hasn't started in full force yet, so I have a minute. Have you looked over the numbers?" I was eager to hear her thoughts.

"I have. I see that you have enough sales and equity in the property that you should be able to get a business loan or an extension on the current loan for expansion."

"That's wonderful news."

"Yeah, you shouldn't have a problem."

"Why do I get the sense there is something else?"

"Well, there are some areas I have questions about. It looks like there are opportunities for you to trim back a little and operate more efficiently from a numbers perspective."

"That sounds like accountant speak for I will not like what you are going to suggest."

"Probably not." She laughed lightheartedly.

"Should we be doing this in person?" I suggested.

"It might be easier if I can show you the numbers I'm talking about and how receptive you are to cost-cutting measures. If you prefer, I can put everything in a report and give it to you when I return your files."

Sarah was being very formal. I wondered how bad her suggestions were going to be and why she was willing just to ship everything over to me via email. I thought about the weekend and tried to remember if I had said or done anything that had offended her.

"Sarah, can I ask you something?"

There was a pause.

I forged on, "are you upset about something?"

"Upset, why would I be upset?" Her voice was higher than normal.

"You sound stressed."

"Work is a little busy at the garden center right now. I am interviewing potential new employees, so are the other departments and there is a lot of paperwork involved. And I've been trying to help Penn with the rest of the wedding arrangements, which reminds me, where are you with the seating chart?"

"I have it done. We can go over it if you want the next time, we get together to discuss the business plan or if you prefer, I can email it to you."

"Email it to me first and then we can talk about it if we need to."

Her words stung me. I had a lot to do myself. Why was I getting upset that she didn't want to spend time with me, neither of us had a lot of free time right now.

"Okay, want to set a meeting for Saturday morning, tentatively," I asked.

"That sounds good but make it early. I've got to go with Eryn and Penn in the afternoon for one last fitting of the dresses."

"Okay. Is eight early enough?"

"That works for me."

"I'll email you the seating chart in just a minute."

"Thanks, see you Saturday."

My phone beeped, indicating she had ended the call. There was a definite coolness in her voice that hadn't been there before. I stared at my phone for the longest time, trying to determine why the shift. Was she really that stressed at her current job?

I spent the day replaying every conversation I had recently with Sarah, trying to find the reason for her attitude today. This is why I don't need serious relationships, always having to wonder if the other person is upset about something you said or didn't say. It was maddening and I found it put me in a foul mood I couldn't shake.

Blue came in around six o'clock, which was early for him. He sat down at the bar and ordered a drink; Brandon sent me a text letting me know he was there.

The kitchen was busy with the dinner crowd and Blue's timing was off, but I went out to say hello to him, anyway.

"Hey man, what are you doing here so early? I asked as soon as I spotted Blue.

"Just stopped by on my way home for a beer and a few minutes of the game."

"Things are a little hectic right now so I can't talk." I looked around the bar at all the occupied tables.

"Okay, well I can still drink a beer, right? Blue asked.

"Yeah man, do whatever you want. I have to get back to the kitchen." I turned and left without waiting for a reply.

When the dinner rush was over, I went back out to the bar to check on things, and Blue was still sitting there. I looked over at Brandon, who just shrugged.

"Is that the same beer you were drinking before?" I asked as I approached.

"No, this is different." Blue leveled a stare at me that I couldn't break. He didn't say anything but then he didn't have to. Blue had a way of asking questions without ever saying a word.

"Brandon, taking care of you?" I didn't know what else to say.

"Always."

I couldn't take this treatment from Blue, and we both knew that he realized something was going on with me. I didn't want to tell him, and he clearly would not leave until I did.

"Listen, about earlier," I started.

Blue just stared at me. He didn't offer any words of support that would prevent me from having to tell him the whole story.

"You want to talk about this somewhere else?" he asked.

"Yeah, come on." I led him back to my office off the kitchen. "Have a seat." I closed the door behind us.

Blue had left his beer at the bar, so I opened my desk drawer and took out a bottle of scotch. "Want a taste?"

"Yeah." He nodded.

I grabbed two glasses off the shelf and poured us each two fingers.

I handed the glass to Blue and raised my own in a toast. "Those we lost."

Blue touched his glass to mine. "May they rest easy."

We each took a drink. I drained my glass and set it on the desk.

Blue was watching me closely. Finally, just when I couldn't take the silence and those eyes piercing me, he spoke.

"Nightmares?"

I just sat there for a minute wondering how much I was going to admit, but who was I kidding? There was no hiding the truth from my friend. He was going to get it one way or the other.

"Yeah, nightmares."

"Same but different?" He asked.

Damn, he was good, and I hated him for it at the moment. I narrowed my gaze.

"I'll take that as a yes," he said before I could say anything.

"Yeah, something like that." I didn't like letting him know he was right. But what did it matter? What was I protecting?

"So, what's the twist?" he rotated his glass around in his hand.

"It's the same old dream but a new face that doesn't belong in there."

Blue studied me for a minute. "Do you want to talk about it?"

"I don't know, I do but I don't want you to accuse me of something that isn't true at the moment."

"No judgment," he held up his hands.

"I'm serious, I don't want you assuming things."

"I can't assume anything if you don't tell me what the hell is going on with you."

"Fine," I said more forcefully than I needed to.

Blue waited.

I ran my hand over my head before getting the courage to tell him about the dream.

"Okay, so it's the same dream about the bomb that went off in the market that day, you remember?" I knew he would, those of us who survived would always remember whether we wanted to or not.

Blue simply nodded for me to continue.

"Well, now I'm lying there staring at the arm like always, but this time when I look up at the sky, I see Sarah's face and she is telling me everything is going to be okay," I paused and shuddered at the thought. I looked up at Blue. "Before you say anything, I am not in a relationship with Sarah. I don't want to be in a relationship with Sarah or anyone for that matter."

Blue just sat there for a long moment and rubbed his five o'clock shadow.

"I don't know what to tell you. If you have no feelings for her, there has to be a reason she is popping up in your dream. Maybe it is a premonition or something."

"Maybe," that was even more disturbing than my previous theories about the change in the dream.

"Maybe it is a good sign." Blue offered.

"How could this be a good sign?"

"Could mean your brain is allowing you to move on. It isn't a memory as much as it is an actual dream influence by what is going on around you and you have been spending a lot of time with Sarah lately. You offered her a job so that is significant in a non-romantic way."

"You may have a point." I was feeling relieved.

"Is that all that is bothering you?"

"Yeah, that's it." I lied. But I wasn't going to confess my struggling with my thoughts of Sarah while I was fully awake.

"You can tell me, man. I won't give you a hard time or judge you if you got something else going on and you want to talk. I will listen."

"Thanks, maybe another night."

Blue nodded and stood up. "I mean it, call me."

"I will." I shook his hand, and he left. I wondered how many of the guys from our unit called him. How much weight was he still carrying on his shoulders?

Chapter 10
Sarah

I got home exhausted as if I had been working all night and it seemed like the moment my head hit the pillow my alarm was beeping incessantly. I turned the weather channel on before getting out of bed. The furnace was on and the ticker scrolling across the bottom of the screen said it was thirty-eight degrees outside. The urge to stay in bed was almost overwhelming. I wanted to lie there going over in my mind how exciting the weekend had been. I looked at the clock one last time and sighed I needed to get moving if I wasn't going to be late.

"Morning Sarah." Eryn greeted me as I came in the door.

"Morning."

Eryn frowned. "You, okay? You don't seem like your normal happy self today."

"I am just tired of this cold, wet weather. I think it is getting to me. Is it ever going to end?"

"I hope so and I doubt Penn has a fur-lined version of my wedding dress." Eryn giggled.

"Oh, I'm sorry, I didn't mean to sound negative; I'm sure the weather will turn nice for your big day."

"Sarah, I'll be just as married, no matter if the sun shines or if it snows. I'm not worried about it."

I sank down in my chair behind the desk, "How can you be so calm? I would be a nervous wreck."

"The only thing that makes me nervous is all the silly details. I'm not nervous about actually getting married, although I probably should be. But the rest it doesn't matter, rain, sun, snow. If people like the food or they don't, the point of the whole thing is sharing a special moment with friends and family. I'd be happy doing this in flip-flops with a crab boil."

I laughed. "Yeah, you probably would. So why are you going through all of this?"

Eryn sighed and sat in a guest chair. "I don't know because it is expected. Because it makes Penn happy?"

"Have you seen Penn lately? She is less than happy, and who cares about Penn? This day is for you and Blue. No one else matters. You have to want it, it needs to reflect who you are, not what everyone else wants or what some bridal magazine says you have to do."

Eryn popped up out of the chair, "You're right. I'm going to call Blue."

I sat there for a minute and then panicked, "Wait! What are you going to do?" If Penn found out that I had talked Eryn out of a wedding ceremony, she would strangle me.

"Blue, it's me. Call me later." Eryn was hanging up the phone by the time I got to her office.

"Are you canceling the wedding?"

"No, of course not. I'm just not sure we need all this fuss. We can keep the reception; we just need to send updated invitations."

"Are you kidding me? Penn is going to absolutely kill me!"

Eryn laughed, "Why, if she isn't having any fun planning the wedding, then why do it?"

"Oh, no!" I started backing out of the office. "I'm not getting in the middle of this with you and Penn. No way!"

I escaped back down the hall to my office and tried to concentrate on the new hire paperwork. I couldn't get the image of the blonde server clinging to Chuck as he gave her a ride on his motorcycle. Why was I even thinking about it? It has nothing to do with me and Chuck's personal life was none of my business. But I couldn't seem to get rid of the image. I tried to focus on work.

The next morning, I got up early and dressed casually. I didn't plan on changing between the meeting with Chuck and the dress fitting, so

I put on loafers, jeans, and an Oxford shirt. I dressed it up a bit with some jewelry. This would have to do for today it was Saturday, after all.

When I arrived at the restaurant, Chuck's motorcycle was parked in the same place as last time. There was another car in the parking lot as well. I wondered who he'd be giving a ride to today. Then I shook the idea from my head. It was none of my business, and I didn't care.

I walked inside and headed back towards the kitchen. I called out Chuck's name.

"In the kitchen, come on in."

I stepped through the swinging door to see Chuck cooking at the griddle. He looked up when I came in.

"Hey good morning, I can make breakfast, unless you already ate?"

"No, I haven't." I shook my head. Why was he always trying to feed me? "You really don't have to do this."

One of the kitchen staff, Derek, came out of the freezer. "Don't bother arguing with him. He isn't happy unless he is shoving food into someone," he said as he put a box down on the counter.

"I like to keep my friends happy and well-fed. Is that a crime?" Chuck called out.

I smiled at Derek.

"I hope you like bacon and eggs." Derek winked.

"I'll choke them down." I smiled back.

"Come on, let's get out of his way," Chuck said grabbing two plates loaded with eggs, bacon, and biscuits."

"But isn't Derek hungry?"

"No, I fed him an hour ago."

Derek nodded and gave me a wink.

"Okay, is that pork?"

Chuck froze. "You don't eat pork?"

"I do, I just haven't had any in a really long time."

"Why, is it a religious preference?"

"No, it's a waistline preference."

Chuck stopped and looked me up and down. My cheeks reddened under his scrutiny.

"You'll be okay." He pushed the door open and led the way to a booth.

I sat down as he placed a plate of more breakfast food than I eat in a week down in front of me.

"Are you serious? I can't eat all of this."

"It isn't as filling as it looks, but no worries if you can't. I'll finish it for you." He sat down with his own plate.

"Shall we talk numbers while we eat?" I asked.

"Why not, I realize you have a schedule to keep."

"Yes, and apparently I'm going to have to hit the gym on the way to the dress fitting." I laughed lightly. "If I don't fit in that dress Penn will kill me."

"You'll be fine. Trust me."

Again, the blood was rising in my cheeks as Chuck's less than subtle gaze raked over me for a second time.

I pulled out my laptop, and the files that Chuck had provided. Then took a bite of the egg.

It was just a scrambled egg, except it wasn't. It was the best scrambled egg I had ever had in my life.

"Mmmm."

"You like it?" Chuck asked with a grin.

"Do you always make your eggs like this?"

"Yes, just your basic scrambled egg."

"What do you do to it?"

"Can't tell you that."

"So, it's a secret egg recipe?" I laughed a little.

"Exactly. Known only to a few."

"I see." I took a bite of the bacon and closed my eyes. It was heavenly. I hadn't had a proper home-cooked breakfast in ages. If

Chuck had offered me the job again and agreed to pay me in food, at that moment I would have taken him up on it.

"Okay, numbers," I said, trying to get back to business.

"Numbers." He agreed with an amused smile.

"You are spending a lot of money on food and ingredients. I don't know enough to understand if there is anything that can be cost savings there."

"Not really. I mean, I could buy cheaper wholesale food, but then they wouldn't be fresh and certainly not local. Those eggs you're eating come from a farm in Chesapeake, they are free-range happy chickens. The bacon came directly from Smithfield. I buy honey from a few suppliers in Gloucester, and I believe it makes a difference in how my food tastes and it also keeps local farmers in business."

"Okay, I see your point there. What about raising your prices?"

Chuck leaned back for a moment and studied me, "let's put a pin in that for the moment and come back to it."

"Okay, fair enough, what about staffing?"

"Staffing?"

"You pay benefits or offer additional monies for health insurance for each full-time employee. Now I can understand providing those benefits for the professional kitchen staff, but not the servers, bartenders, and dishwashers.

Chuck frowned, "they all aren't full time."

"No, not all of them, but if you made a few more of them part-time so you didn't have to cover the cost of the benefits and extra hours...."

"I'd have more employees to make up the difference in hours, and they would be less loyal to me knowing they could get part-time work anywhere. Not every restaurant hires full-time staff."

"Okay, but I'm just saying you could be more efficient. What about the bar?"

"Well, the hard liquor has to be purchased from the state, so there isn't any cost-cutting to be done there. I might save on some beer and wine which I can get at a more wholesale price, but again."

"You buy local," I added for him.

He nodded, "Now you're catching on."

"Then the only thing left to do is apply to the bank."

"Do we have everything we need?"

"Yes, want to do it now?" I asked.

Chuck took a deep breath. "Yes."

"Okay." I brought up the bank's website and let Chuck log into his account. He found the tab for business loans and half an hour later, he had completed his application.

Chuck sat back in the booth and let out a sigh. "Thank you so much for your help."

"I didn't really do much."

"Well, another set of eyes is always helpful, and just being here made the process less intimidating."

I wasn't sure what to do, so I just nodded.

"Hey, Chuck!"

I recognized that all too perky voice.

"Hi Brittany, you're here early."

"Yeah, I wanted to come by and talk to you."

"I'll give you some privacy." I slid out of my seat.

"Oh no, you can stay," Brittany generously said.

"You know my car broke down."

Chuck nodded.

"Well, I'm going to have to get a new one and that is going to take me a while to save up the money."

"I can imagine," Chuck said.

I watched with fascination, wondering if she was about to ask him for a loan of her own.

"As you know, I live across town and it takes too long to get here by bus, so I found another job closer to my apartment."

I sat stunned. I don't know what I was expecting, but it wasn't to be a witness to perky Brittany resigning.

"I understand, of course; you can always come back when you're ready," Chuck said graciously.

"Thanks, I'm so glad you understand."

"Use me as a reference if you need to," Chuck offered.

"Thanks, you're the best." Brittany smiled at me and then turned and left.

Chuck raised his eyebrows at me. "Well, that was unexpected."

"Was she full time or part-time?" I asked, bringing the laptop back to life.

Chuck laughed. "Sarah, you're amazing!"

"What? I'm serious."

"Okay, she was part time."

"Do you need to replace her?"

"I can try it without her for a week if that makes you happy."

"Okay, try it and see if you can manage; you might save a little money."

"She was a very popular server. People used to request to sit in her section all the time."

"I bet," I said, leveling a stare at him.

He didn't comment but tilted his head and lifted an eyebrow at me.

Chapter 11
Sarah

I met Eryn, and Penn at Penn's boutique for our final fitting Saturday afternoon.

The dresses were simple and elegant, nothing lacy, nothing over the top for Eryn. It was one thing she made sure she had a say in. Otherwise, she would have been flouncing down the aisle in whatever the latest style in Paris was this spring, which I'm sure would-be nothing Eryn would be caught dead in. Penn and I had matching dresses, a pale blue sheath that was low cut in the front and gathered in the back.

Eryn was stunning in the white silk sleeveless sheath with a brocade bodice and a deep V in both the front and back. There was just the hint of a train.

I envisioned a sprig of baby's breath in her hair for a perfect touch. But Eryn wasn't having it. She said it was impractical for an outdoor wedding along the water and she was probably right. She'd just worry about the thing flying off during the ceremony.

I gushed over her as she stepped out from the dressing room. "Eryn, that is breath-taking. I can tell you I have wasted my time planning a reception because when Blue sees you in that he is going to whisk you away to your honeymoon as soon as the ceremony ends."

She smiled at herself in the full-length mirror. "It is beautiful, Penn. Thank you."

I was getting misty eyed as Penn, and Eryn hugged.

"Let's see you in your dress, Penn." I demanded.

"Why, it looks just like yours."

I scoffed, "I bet not!" Penn and I were about the same height and while we both were slender; Penn had a few more pronounced curves than I did. She had a lighter skin tone, and I was eager to see the dress on her.

Penn disappeared for a moment. When she returned, I saw I was right; Penn filled her dress out way better than I ever could.

"That isn't fair, you are prettier than the bride!" Eryn fussed.

Penn waived her hand dismissively. "No one is going to be looking at me."

"Are you bringing a date?" I asked Penn.

"I doubt it. Seems a little too gauche."

I nodded and wondered if she was still mourning the breakup with Richard.

"What about you, Sarah?" Eryn asked.

"A date? Are you kidding? Definitely not."

"It doesn't have to be a romantic date, bring a friend." Eryn offered.

"Bring Chuck." Penn added.

I frowned. "Chuck will be there; it is his restaurant." I reminded her.

Eryn looked from me to Penn, "Chuck?"

"No, there is no *Chuck*," I emphasized.

"I bet there could be if you wanted there to be." Penn wiggled her eyebrows.

"No, I don't want there to be, a Chuck or a Dave or anyone else. Second, I am not Chuck's type."

"Wait, what am I missing?" Eryn asked.

"Nothing, there is nothing to miss except Penn's imagination running wild."

"Penn...." Eryn scolded.

"What? She is helping him out, and they spend a lot of time together. I'm just saying he's a red-blooded male, I'm sure, he wouldn't need much encouragement from Sarah if she wanted more than a business relationship with him."

"But I don't want more and trust me when I tell you I am not his type."

Penn and Eryn exchanged looks, and both came to stand in front of me with their arms crossed.

"What happened?" They said in unison.

"Nothing happened, less than nothing happened. We should probably change out of these dresses before they get ruined." I said, trying to regain some control of the situation. Penn I could handle, but Eryn and Penn I'm not so sure I could withstand the tag team.

"Fine." Penn turned on her heel and disappeared to change. I returned to the dressing room up front where I had left my clothes. Eryn did the same.

Both Erin and Penn were waiting for me when I finally emerged. I had hoped by taking a little extra time, the two of them would forget about me and move on to the more important topics of discussion.

"So where are we going for lunch?"

"How about the Crab Shack?" Eryn suggested.

I was relieved. It was a wonderful restaurant on the fishing pier upriver from Chuck's place.

"Sounds good, they have a wonderful view, and it is a nice day."

We all agreed to drive separately. Once in my car, I cranked up the radio.

We were halfway through the oysters on the half shell when Penn brought up the subject of Chuck again.

"So, tell me how this weekend was with Chuck."

"I told you the other night." I protested this line of inquiry.

"All you said was that it was chaos and something about the kitchen staff, nothing about Chuck."

"Because other than what I've already told you, there isn't anything about 'Chuck' to tell."

Eryn and Penn each pegged me with a stare.

"What? I enjoyed the weekend. Watching Chuck and the staff work last Sunday was amazing, the restaurant was controlled chaos. Chuck gave me copies of his financials for me to go over and he walked me to the door when I left."

"Did you meet any of the other staff?"

"Sure, he introduced me to everyone, and a server named Brittany, I believe that was her name."

"You didn't really catch her name?" Penn smiled and leaned forward, elbows on the table.

"And what did this Brittany look like?"

"I didn't really pay that much attention."

"Hmmm, I see." Penn pretended to be interested while stirring her drink.

"And why would he only introduce you to one member of the wait staff and not all of them?"

Eryn leaned forward "What do you mean 'you didn't pay attention'?"

"I mean, she was talking to Chuck, and I was concentrating on my work."

"So, you didn't notice anything about her?" Penn asked.

"Nothing, I'm serious you two need a life. Brittany came over to confirm Chuck was going to give her a ride on his motorcycle after work, or something. Again, I wasn't paying attention."

Both Eryn and Penn leaned back in the booth.

"And did Chuck confirm it?" Eryn asked.

"Confirm what?" I said, a little too defensively.

"That he would give her a ride?"

"Oh yeah, I guess so. Like I said, I wasn't listening all that closely."

Just then our server arrived with the entrees, and we dropped the subject of Brittany.

What did I care if he gave an employee a ride on his bike? Maybe she needed a ride home and it was all that innocent. It would be a gracious thing to do. Besides, she was gone anyway, so it didn't matter. Not that it ever did.

Penn ordered dessert for us, despite my and Eryn's protests.

"What are your plans for this weekend?" Penn asked me.

"I don't really have any plans. Why?"

"Are you going to see Chuck again?"

"I saw him this morning."

"What?" Eryn and Penn both gaped at me.

"What's the big deal? I gave him his financials back and shared with him some cost cutting ideas. I told him I would help him change his business plan if he wanted to, and then I helped him fill out the loan application online."

"And you're just now telling us this?" Penn sat her fork down next to the cheesecake.

I stared at her plate for a moment, remembering the cheesecake Chuck had sent home with me.

"So how did things go this morning?" Eryn asked, taking a bite of her cobbler.

"It was okay. I suggested he convert a few more full-time positions to part time so he could save on salary and benefits."

"I bet you did." Penn laughed.

"What did he say?" Eryn ignored Penn.

"The idea didn't thrill him, and he said he would need those positions even more when he added the food truck catering to the business. But one of his employees quit while I was there so, if he doesn't replace her that might save him a little money." I sighed, "I told him it was certainly his choice not mine and hopefully the expansion would bring in enough money to cover the expenses of the full-time staff."

"Makes sense." Eryn nodded. "Is he planning on running the restaurant and the catering side of things?"

"Initially he wants to, but frankly I don't see how he can. Hopefully, he will realize that sooner rather than later he will need some help."

"Has he offered you a job yet?" Eryn asked.

I stared at her blankly and then shifted my eyes to Penn.

"Don't look at me, I didn't say anything."

"He did, didn't he?" Eryn sat back away from the table.

I nodded, "He did, and I turned him down."

"Why?" She looked at me in disbelief.

"Because I have a job."

"So?"

I stared, slacked jawed, at Eryn.

Eryn leaned in again. "Don't take this the wrong way, but you have to take opportunities when they come along."

"What if I find I don't like the food industry, what if I am completely happy working for you?"

"Then you should continue working for me if that is how you feel, but I hope you have more ambition than to be my office manager for the rest of your life, you're too young for that."

I had the urge to argue; I considered telling her that if I was happy doing what I was doing, then isn't that what life was all about. That money, promotions, and all that other stuff didn't matter? But I couldn't. I couldn't form the words in my mouth, and I knew Eryn understood.

Chapter 12
Chuck

The weekend seemed to fly by too quickly. People had flocked to the Seabreeze to sit out on the deck and take in the sun. The forecast was promising continued warm temperatures for the rest of the week. I knew the dinner crowd would be busier this week, and I was preparing for it.

I came out of the kitchen and found Blue sitting at the bar. "Hey man, what's up?"

"Nothing much, just stopped by to see how things are going with you."

"Couldn't be better, business is booming, it is almost more than I can handle some nights."

Blue looked around. It was busy with people enjoying March Madness basketball, their eyes glued to the TV screens above the bar.

"Maybe, you need more help." Blue suggested slyly.

"Yeah, more help cost money and I am walking a thin line right now trying to expand."

"If you can't handle the business you have, how are you going to expand?"

"I'll have to rearrange some schedules. I'll work it out."

"Sounds like you need someone to help you."

I knew what Blue was hinting at; I shook my head. "Look, I already told you she turned me down," I argued.

"She didn't totally turn you down; she is helping you part time."

"True. What are you getting at?" I wondered why we were having this conversation again. "Wait, she told Eryn, didn't she?"

"Something like that."

"Is Eryn mad at me?"

"No, she told Sarah to take the job."

I stopped wiping the counter to stare at Blue. "She did what?"

"Eryn told Sarah not to let good opportunities pass her by."

"What did Sarah say?"

"Oh, no! I'm not getting in the middle of this. I honestly don't know what Sarah said. But I can't believe you are trying to sabotage my marriage before it even starts."

"What the hell are you talking about?"

"You realize Eryn is a workaholic already. If she loses Sarah, she'll be back to doing the financials on her own again and I'll never see her."

"Okay, whoa! I'm sure if, and I mean if, Sarah agreed to come work for me, which she has not, she wouldn't leave Eryn hanging like that and would hire a replacement before she left."

"You're probably right, Sarah is a really terrific girl."

"Yeah, she is."

"So, you are interested in her." Blue pointed a finger in my direction.

"No, I'm not. At least not in any way other than an employee."

"Sarah is very attractive." Blue pointed out the obvious.

"She is," I agreed. "But again, I'm not flirting with her, and I don't want to date her. Haven't we had this conversation already?"

"Yeah, something along these lines."

"But you think if you keep asking me the same question, you'll get a different answer?"

Blue grinned. "Works sometimes."

"On criminals, not on me."

"On everyone. I gotta run." Blue got up to leave.

"Alright, wanna go fishing this weekend or something?"

"Yeah, let's do that and catch a game afterward," Blue suggested.

"Okay, see ya."

I headed back to the kitchen to check on things. Blue had several good points, but Sarah had made it pretty clear she was all business. I could respect that. But I didn't want to. It made little sense. Sarah was very attractive, smart, and serious. She was not a party girl and not someone who seemed to be interested in short-term relationships, in other words, not my type. So why did it bother me so much that Sarah didn't seem to be attracted to me? One thing I was sure of, is that I wasn't interested in a long-term relationship that would inevitably end in disaster. Too many of my friends had been down that road, even Blue had been married before. No, I had too much baggage of my own. I didn't need to burden anyone else with it, and I certainly didn't need to take on anyone else's. No short term, good time relationships were better.

What I needed right now was to focus on something else for a while. I was losing the urge to create anything new in the kitchen. I had at least a week, if not more, before I would hear from the bank. And I found my weekends were not nearly as exciting without coffee first thing in the morning with Sarah. I hated to admit it, but it was true. Maybe there wasn't anything romantic between us, but I still liked her company. She was easy to talk to, and her eyes told you everything she was thinking even when her mouth didn't. With one project on hold until I heard from the bank, I needed something else to keep my brain occupied. And that would have to be Blue's bachelor party. I made a mental note to work on that tonight after the restaurant closed.

I knew Blue would invite the guys from our unit, but I wasn't sure who had responded yet. I sent a text to Sarah.

"I need your help once again; can you share with me the guest list?"

A few minutes went by before I received a reply.

"Sure, do you need a final count?"

"This is for the bachelor party so just need to know which of Blue's friends RSVP'd."

"I'll let you know tomorrow. I will have to get the list from Penn."

"Okay."

Well, I could do a little planning tonight and reach out to the guys tomorrow. Blue wasn't going to want any of the traditional stuff; we'd all done that before when he got married the first time and we were all much younger. No, this was going to have to be fun and tasteful. I went to my office and got on the computer and started searching the internet for ideas. I was thinking maybe deep-sea fishing or golf. A private party here afterwards? I needed to know who was coming before I could settle on any one idea. Not all the guys played golf since a couple had mobility issues. So, I needed to plan accordingly. I probably should have done this a month ago, but where was the fun in that?

Chapter 13

Sarah

It was Wednesday, and the week was dragging on. We were getting shipments in, but the customers hadn't started shopping in earnest yet. Eryn said that things would pick up soon. But this lull was making me crazy. All the plans for the wedding reception were in place, Chuck had submitted his loan proposal to the bank, so he didn't currently need my help. Suddenly it was as if I had too much free time on my hands. Maybe I would call Penn and see if she needed any help.

"Hey, everything okay?" Eryn asked, as she popped her head into my office.

"Yeah, everything is great."

"Your words say 'great', but your tone says, things could be better." Eryn came in and sat down in the plastic chair across from my desk.

"I probably shouldn't say this to my boss, there is probably some unwritten code out there or something, but I'm bored. I was overworked for a while and now that the reception is under control, Chuck's waiting to hear from the bank, and the new hires are on board, I'm feeling a little useless."

Eryn laughed, "It's okay to say you are bored. This isn't the most riveting of jobs, I realize that. But the fact that you handled this job with added responsibilities and organized a wedding reception and helped a friend tells me you have one hell of a work ethic and are good at what you do because it all got done. And here you are, turning into a workaholic."

I smiled. "It was a stressful time, and I got addicted to the stress."

"It is easy to do." Eryn agreed. "Do you want to take the afternoon off?"

"That is nice of you to offer, but what would I do? I have no place I need to be, no friends in need of my help."

Eryn looked sympathetic. "Why don't you do something for yourself? Why don't you go to a movie, or a museum? Take a walk along one of the nature trails?"

I looked at her dubiously. She, of course, had a point, I could go do any of those things. But it was a sad commentary on my life that I would have to do them alone. I hadn't kept in touch with the girls I had worked with at the accounting firm. Because of Rob, the crazy stalker from the IT department, I had to cut all ties. My friends were Penn and Eryn, and neither of them was going to be up for a day of nature trails. Penn would be good for lunch and a manicure, but honestly, I wasn't in the mood for the drama that came with Penn today. My mind floated to Chuck, but he wasn't likely to take off from the restaurant in the middle of the day to go do whatever with me. And not a good idea if I was trying to keep things professional between us. I sighed heavily.

"I need a new social life."

Eryn looked at me puzzled, "I'll try not to take that personally."

"I just mean that if I were to take the afternoon off as you suggested, I don't have a friend available to go do any of those things with me. So, what's the point?"

"Wow, you have it bad." Eryn stood up and fished out her walkie-talkie and called out to the greenhouses. "Brad, I'm taking a vacation day. You're in charge."

Brad's voice crackled over the radio. "Repeat that, please."

"I'm going to be gone for the rest of the day, you're in charge."

"10-4."

I sat staring at Eryn.

"Well, come on." She motioned for me to follow her.

I grabbed my purse and turned off my computer rushing to follow her.

"What are you doing?"

"You need a break. Lord knows I need one too."

"Are we going to give Penn a call?"

"No, we can do without miss high and mighty today," Eryn grinned.

"Where are we going?" I asked, trying to keep up as Eryn headed to the parking lot.

"The beach, get in." she said, unlocking her car.

"I realize we have had a couple of warm days lately, but it isn't quite beach weather, is it?"

"It is always beach weather, when you have a wet suit."

I slid into the passenger seat. "Why do we need a wet suit?"

"Because I am going to teach you to surf." Eryn put the car in gear, and we drove out of the parking lot.

"You've gone bonkers."

"You can swim, can't you?"

"Yeah, but..."

"But nothing. We'll stop by my house and change; grab a couple of suits and boards and we can be in the water in an hour."

"I'm not so sure about this, Eryn." I was suddenly regretting having said anything.

"Of course not. Because you've never done it before. You need a distraction, and you need something to break up the ordinary. Surfing is the answer, trust me."

"Okay." I said but wasn't so sure.

A few minutes later we were at Eryn's, and she was tossing swim shorts and t-shirts at me. I changed into the swimwear and put my clothes back on over it for warmth. It might be sixty degrees, but to me that was not warm enough for shorts and a t-shirt.

I followed her down to the garage and helped her grab a couple of surfboards and strap them to the roof of her car.

We were back on the road, headed to Virginia Beach in a matter of minutes.

"Eryn, are you sure about this?" I asked once we were standing on the sand holding the boards.

"It will be fine."

"I keep having thoughts of having to be dragged from the surf by a lifeguard or something."

"Oh, there's no need to worry about that, there are no lifeguards this time of year." She grinned. "Come on, we won't go out far, and I'll get you acclimated to the board. Trust me."

I followed Eryn to the water's edge. She left her board in the sand and took me out into the water about waist deep.

"Get familiar with the board and how the water moves so that you can learn balance. Let the board become an extension of your body. So, hop up here and lay on your belly." She smiled.

Eryn held the board steady as I made a couple of attempts at getting on. When I finally made it, Eryn cheered.

"That's it, that is the hardest part."

"I doubt that." I looked at her, wondering why I had never realized she was crazy until now.

Eryn pushed me into a spot for the next set of waves coming in. "Okay, so just stay down on the board, don't stand yet and just ride the wave towards shore."

I looked behind me. I never thought the waves in Virginia Beach were enormous, not compared to pictures of waves in other places, but suddenly they looked terrifying.

"Eryn, are you sure about this?"

"I'll be right beside you the whole time." She looked over her shoulder, "Hang on!"

Something suddenly pushed me away from Eryn, and I screamed. When the water got too shallow, I rolled off the board awkwardly.

"That was perfect!" Eryn clapped, standing beside me.

"It didn't feel perfect." I said, taking advantage of the water ebbing to stand up.

"Want to do it again?"

I looked back at the waves and smiled. "Yeah!"

"Okay, this time I'll get my board and you do what I do, okay?"

"Okay."

We repeated the process a few more times, then Eryn decided it was time for me to learn to stand. I started questioning my own sanity at this point. But Eryn was patient, and we laughed each time I fell off the board. Finally, I made it all the way back to the shallow water without falling off. It wasn't graceful, but I did it.

When I lowered myself onto the board and then straddled it like Eryn showed me, I heard clapping and whistles from the beach. I was mortified to see a small crowd of people had formed, some of them with boards cheering me on.

"Oh my god, Eryn!" I suddenly felt very exposed.

"You were amazing! You'll be a pro in no time!"

"Why didn't you tell me people were watching?"

"Why would I do that?"

I frowned. A couple of guys paddled out to where we were sitting.

The first one to reach us said, "Hey, you did really great!"

A moment later his friend joined, "Mind if we share your waves?"

"Yeah, no problem." Eryn nodded.

I shot Eryn an expression that screamed, 'why are you doing this to me'? But she only laughed and turned her board around. I tried to do the same but was struggling a little when one of the guys, a blonde with a shark's tooth necklace hanging out of the top of his wetsuit, reached over and gave me a hand.

"Thanks," I mumbled.

"No worries. You'll get the hang of it." He flashed a perfectly white smile and paddled away to catch the next wave.

I don't know how long we were out there, but I was getting tired, and my brain was fuzzy. Eryn waved for me to follow her, and we paddled back to the beach.

"How do you feel?"

I leaned against Eryn's car.

"Sore and tired."

"I shouldn't have kept you out there so long. Here." She handed me a bottle of water and I drank it down without stopping.

Eryn smiled. "Want another?"

"Yes, please."

I drank this one more slowly and watched the remaining surfers in the water.

"Did you like it?" Eryn asked cautiously.

"Yes, I did actually. I mean it was nerve-wracking and kinda scary but also fun."

She nodded, "Good."

We put the boards back on her car and headed back to the garden center so I could get my car. "I'll follow you back to your place and help you put all of this away." I offered.

"You don't have to help me do this Sarah; I can see that you're tired. And this is going to take a while."

"I can't just leave you to do the work."

"Yes, you can. I need to strip and wax the boards; I've been putting it off for a while and after today, I need to strip these before we go out again. It is very therapeutic for me, really. You can go home and get some rest."

I got the impression she really wanted to be alone, so I agreed and drove home. I decided a nice soak in the tub is what my cold, aching muscles needed.

The next day my muscles were stiff, but I felt better and more energized. Surfing had been just what I needed.

Eryn bounced in my office with a smile and a radiance that said the surfing had been good for her, too.

"Hey Sarah, did you get an invitation from Chuck for St. Patrick's Day?"

"I did last night, but I was too tired to respond. Did you get a text too?"

"He sent the invite to Blue. You gonna go? We could invite Penn and make it a genuine party."

"If all of you are going, then I'm in." I hadn't responded to the text because I felt uncomfortable going alone. I was still struggling with my attraction to Chuck. So far, I had kept my promise to myself about not dating but going alone to a party he was hosting could complicate things.

Eryn gave me a puzzled look, but I ignored it. I didn't want to get into my conflicting opinions about Chuck. Having to discuss it with Penn was bad enough.

I took out my phone and hit reply. "I'll be there."

Chapter 14
Sarah

Penn and I drove together to the Seabreeze; agreeing to meet Blue and Eryn there.

"Wow, there are a million cars, there is no way we are going to find a place to park." Penn observed as we drove around looking for a spot.

I pointed. "That guy over there is waving to us." Penn pulled over to a young man in a server's uniform. As she lowered her car window, the young man leaned down.

"Are you Penn and Sarah?"

"Yes, we are. Can you direct us where we can park?" Penn asked.

"Right over here." The young man pointed and started walking in the direction of the back of the restaurant.

There was a parking space with an orange cone in it and a handwritten sign that read 'Reserved for Penn and Sarah'.

Penn looked over at me with raised eyebrows, "If you're not interested in Chuck maybe, I'll date him, he's got class."

I snorted. "Be my guest."

But the words were bitter on my tongue; I didn't like the idea of Penn dating Chuck. And it wasn't because then I'd have to hear endless conversations about Chuck, did this or Chuck did that. I'd seen how Penn treated men. I would really hate to see her treat him that way, not that he would allow it. As soon as we were parked, the young man was waiting for us and led us inside through a staff door, avoiding the throngs of people crowded around the bar.

"Thank you." Penn said as she handed him a generous tip. "Thank you, ma'am." He pocketed the money and disappeared into the crowd.

I could see Eryn waving to us from a high-top table along the back wall. "Penn! Sarah!"

"Good lord, there are twice as many people as there are cars!" Penn groused.

I nodded and politely pushed our way over to the table.

"Wow, Chuck wasn't kidding when he said it was going to be a party!" I exclaimed.

Blue raised his mug of green beer. "If it is one thing Chuck knows how to do, it's how to throw a party."

Penn slid into the chair closest to the wall so she would have a better view of the room. A moment later, a server appeared with a mug for me and a glass of wine for Penn. "Snacks will be out in a minute."

Penn looked at the wine. "How did she know I didn't drink beer?"

Eryn laughed. "I told her when we got here that our friends would join us, and they would need one beer and one white wine."

Penn winked at Eryn, "You think of everything."

"Yes, I do." Eryn grinned mischievously.

Penn took a sip of her wine, then asked, "Who do we thank for the parking spot?"

"That was Chuck's idea." Eryn smiled.

Penn looked around. "That was nice of him. Where is Mr. Wonderful?"

"Oh, I'm sure he'll be along shortly." Blue reassured her.

It suddenly got quiet in the restaurant as the din of conversation subsided and the band stopped playing. A voice came over the speakers, letting everyone know that the beer mug lift would begin soon.

I looked from Eryn to Blue. "What is a beer mug lift?"

Eryn leaned close so that she could explain, "That is when they give you the largest beer mug, they have. Fill it and you hold it up over your head. The person who can hold their mug up the longest wins."

"You wanna do it?" Blue asked me.

I thought about it for a minute and decided that after learning to surf, I could do anything. "Yeah, let's go! Who's with me?"

Penn rolled her eyes. "I'll pass."

"Okay, watch our purses." Eryn giggled as she and I slid off the bar stool.

"Aren't you coming?" I looked at Blue.

"No, it wouldn't be fair."

Eryn turned to face him. "Why is that?"

"Because I always win. I have powerful arms and shoulders."

"Whatever!" I said and headed for the bar. Eryn was right behind me.

"Ladies!" The bartender greeted us and handed us mugs. "No drinking until the game is over."

"Got it!" We stood, resting our mugs on the edge of a nearby table with some other participants. Chuck came out of the kitchen to stand behind the bar and start the contest. He grabbed the bullhorn.

"Okay everyone, the rules are simple, the last beer in the air wins!" The crowd cheered. "Ready? Beers up!" Eryn and I raised our mugs. The band started playing. Eryn leaned over and whispered in my ear, "concentrate on the music, don't think about the beer."

I nodded. I had waited tables in college, so hopefully my arm strength from lifting all those serving trays hadn't diminished. The first song ended, and a few beers disappeared. The lead singer of the band pointed to those that gave up. They were tagged with a green piece of tape and ushered to the sidelines so that they couldn't reenter the contest. The second song ended, and we both were still going strong. More people were ushered to the side. The band started playing again; Eryn and I began to sing along. The surrounding people joined in, and we were having a wonderful time. The band changed songs, a few more people gave up and finally it was down to just Eryn and me.

It felt like the whole restaurant was watching as the band played, and we sang. I saw Chuck out of the corner of my eye, watching with a smile on his face and his muscular arms crossed over his chest. It was going to be close. It would be hard to beat Eryn as she lifted plants all day long and surfboards with ease. I felt my muscles twitched, and I didn't want to shake and spill beer down on my head. I gritted my teeth and spied the blonde surfer from the beach. He gave me a brief wave and I, lowered my beer. There was a collective groan from the crowd and then a cheer for Eryn.

"How about a round of applause for our new beer lift champion!" Chuck shouted into the bullhorn. The blonde made his way over to me.

"Hey, you surf and almost won the beer lift challenge, I think I'm in love." He smiled a charming smile.

I laughed, "Well, I've only surfed the one time, and I just lost the contest, so I think you can do better."

"No way, I like a woman who isn't afraid to try something new." He flashed another smile with perfectly straight teeth, and his blue eyes crinkled a little in the corners.

It was hard not to smile back. The little voice inside my head was telling me to stay away, that my taste in men was horrible and this guy would likely be no exception. He already knew too much about me; I'd only met him twice, and I knew nothing about him. Knowing my luck, he was probably some sort of surfing serial killer or something. But despite the warnings in my brain, I heard my voice betray me. "Are you here with your friends from the beach?"

"Yeah, you want to come join us?" He looked over his shoulder at his friend.

"I wish I could, but I am here with friends, too. I wouldn't want to be rude, we only just got here. Maybe you can join us? We have a table in the back." I turned to look toward our table, but the crowd partially obscured my view, and I spied Chuck watching me from the end of the bar.

"That's cool." He signaled to his friend.

"I'm Sarah, by the way."

"I'm Brad," he answered, "this is my friend Paul." I nodded, "Hi Paul."

"Hi," Paul said with his own version of a perfect smile and curly sandy blonde hair above deep green eyes.

I sighed to myself; this was going to be a long night.

"Um, we're right over here." I led them through the crowd. When Eryn saw me with the surfers in tow, she cocked an eyebrow and tried not to smile.

"You remember my friend Eryn?" I asked.

"Sure, nice to see you again." Brad smiled.

"Hi, I'm Paul."

Eryn nodded to each of them.

"This is my fiancé` Blue and our friend Penn."

The three men nodded to each other. Both Brad and Paul ogled at Penn. "Hi," they each said breathlessly.

I rolled my eyes, and Eryn giggled into her winning beer.

"Hello." Penn smiled, her eyes dancing with delight.

"Hi, do you surf too?" Paul asked Penn.

"Not in a while, Eryn is the pro."

Brad and Paul turned back to Eryn. She waved her hand. "It was a long time ago, and I won a few championships, but I was never a pro."

"You looked like you knew what you were doing the other day." Brad nodded.

"I still enjoy it."

Blue looked at her curiously. Clearly, she hadn't told him she had skipped work to take me surfing. The server reappeared with potato wedges, fried onion rings, and mushroom caps.

"More beer and wine?"

"Yes, please." I answered.

She disappeared and returned later with Chuck helping her carry all the beer. I felt my heart sink at the sight of him.

"Hey, buddy!" Blue greeted him.

"Looks like you guys have your own party going." Chuck looked around the table.

"We are growing by the minute." Eryn laughed, accepting a new beer, ignoring the look from Blue.

Brad and Paul accepted theirs, Penn smiled as Chuck set the wineglass down in front of her.

"My lady." He smiled at her. Penn looked like a kid in a candy store, with Brad and Paul flanking her.

"You must be Chuck; I've heard a lot about you." She smiled sweetly.

"Really?" Chuck looked from me to Blue. "I'm almost afraid to ask if any of it was good."

"Does it matter?" Penn batted her eyes.

I couldn't take it. "So, Brad, are you from here?" I asked, trying not to watch what was surely going to end in a train wreck by the end of the night.

"No, I came here to go to school. I have a couple more classes and I'll be finished with my master's degree." Penn's ears perked up.

"What is your degree in?" I tried to ignore Penn.

"Master's in Business Administration, Paul, too." Brad thumbed in his friend's direction.

Penn practically licked her lips. I could see the wheels turning in her head. I shot a look to Eryn over the rim of my beer mug. Brad, who was standing between Penn, and I shifted slightly in her direction. I breathed a small sigh of relief.

"You need anything, Sarah?" I jumped. I forgot Chuck was standing behind me out of the aisle so the servers who were running back and forth with food and drink could pass.

"I'm good." I gave him a tight smile.

Chuck put his hand lightly on my shoulder. "Ya'll let me know if you need anything. I need to get back."

Then he disappeared. We laughed, drank, and ate. Eryn, having had more beer than usual, played a few more pub games and lost. Brad and Paul drifted away but promised to see us at the beach. I was relieved when they left and surprised Penn hadn't left with them. Chuck had been back to the table twice to check on us; Penn had flirted with him unabashedly.

I looked across the table at Eryn whose eyes were drooping heavily. "I think Eryn is going to fall asleep."

"Yeah, I think I am going to have to take her home." Blue agreed.

"I'm ready to call it a night myself. What about you Penn?"

"Yeah, I'm ready."

I flagged the server. "Can you bring me our bill; we need to be going."

"Oh, sure. She pulled out her a cell phone and tapped on it. The bill should be up on your screen there, pay when you're ready."

She pointed to a small screen at the edge of the table that I hadn't noticed before.

"Excuse me, are these new?"

"Yeah, we are testing a handful of them out before we commit to the company. Let us know how you like it."

I frowned. Chuck hadn't mentioned these, and there weren't in the financial documents I reviewed for his bank loan. I wondered just how new they were.

"I've got this," Blue said, pulling out his wallet.

"At least let me pay for mine!" I whined.

"No." He stated simply and tapped his credit card on the screen. "And it's too late. Done." He grinned.

I could see why Eryn had fallen for him; he was more handsome than a man had a right to be and when he smiled; it was near perfection as a stray black curl fell over one of those icy blue eyes.

"Now, let's get out of here before Chuck realizes we are leaving. He normally refuses to let me pay." Blue said, gathering Eryn up out of her chair.

I laughed as she flounced against him and smiled. "Do you need help?" I asked.

"No, I'll be fine. Let's slip out the staff door."

Penn and I led the way, and we got to our cars without any protests from Chuck.

Once alone in the car, Penn looked over at me. "So, Eryn took you surfing?"

"Yeah, I was stressed out at work, she took off early and we went to the beach. I was really nervous at first, but it was actually fun."

"And you met Brad and Paul?"

"Yeah, but I didn't even know their names until tonight."

"And you aren't dating either of them."

"I am not and do not plan to date anyone."

"I see."

I wasn't sure if she was asking because she was concerned for my love life or hers.

It surprised me to see a text from Chuck a couple of days later. He hadn't seemed all that talkative on St. Patrick's Day, but then he had been pretty busy that night.

I stared at my phone for a moment, considering his invitation to have dinner. My heart wanted to say yes, but my head said, don't get involved. A customer came in and asked for help. When they had moved on to the greenhouse to browse the plants, I pulled my phone back out. I typed my reply without thinking about it. I just did it. I agreed to meet with him at what I assumed would be his place.

Then, I shoved the phone back in my pocket and tried not to think about the worst that could happen.

I spent the afternoon arguing with myself that despite my track record with men, this could all just be business related, and Chuck may not have any romantic interest in me whatsoever.

"Hey Sarah, you, okay?"

"What?" I looked up to see Eryn watching while I was just standing there lost in thought, staring at a pack of pepper seeds.

"You look like you are zoned out." Eryn laughed.

"Oh, sorry." I looked around, trying to remember what I was doing.

"Something on your mind?"

I sighed. "Can I ask you something kinda personal?"

"Sure, why don't we go into my office."

"Yeah, okay." I started chewing my thumbnail, a bad habit I had never outgrown.

Once we were in the office and had some privacy, Eryn turned to me. "Spill."

"Blue has been friends with Chuck a long time, right?"

She gave me a puzzled look. "Yeah, fifteen years or more."

"And Blue wouldn't be friends with him if he was," I paused, trying to decide if I should even continue. "If Chuck was a bad person, right?"

Eryn leaned back in her chair and studied me for a moment. I felt stupid for asking her.

"I'm sorry, Eryn, I shouldn't have asked you that. I shouldn't have put you in that position to answer that question."

"You like him, don't you?"

"I guess I do." I chewed harder.

"I believe Chuck likes you too."

I raised my eyebrows at her. "I just don't want another stalker situation."

"Listen, I doubt seriously Chuck is perfect. But Blue wouldn't consider him a close friend if he were an evil person with psycho tendencies."

"I suppose not."

"Do you want me to ask him tonight?" Eryn offered.

"No! No, I shouldn't have said anything. Besides, I am seeing Chuck tonight. So, it will be too late." I laughed a little.

"Tonight?"

"Yeah, he sent me a text asking me to meet him at his house." I realized I sounded like a high school girl going on a first date. "I'm sure it is about his business plan or something and I am probably just over thinking this and assuming it is anything else."

Eryn gave me a small smile. "It could be both."

I shook my head in disbelief.

"I saw the way he was watching the two guys from the beach when they were talking to you at the St. Paddy's Day party. If you ask me, he was jealous."

"Jealous?" I whispered and sunk down into Eryn's guest chair to consider her words. "You think so?"

"Just let it happen. You won't know what his intentions are unless you go over there. You have my number and Blue's. If Chuck gets out of hand, leave. If you can't leave, call one of us. But I seriously doubt that is going to be a problem. Chuck seems to be a really nice guy. He plays in charity golf tournaments with Blue, and he is a member of a motorcycle club of wounded vets that do a lot of charity work too. I think you'll be fine."

"Okay, I see your point."

"Yes." Eryn gave me a wicked smile, "But, call me if you find any bodies in the basement."

"You're awful!" I laughed and refocused on work.

Chapter 15
Chuck

St. Patrick's Day was a bigger success than I thought it would be this year, so I didn't have time to talk to Sarah and celebrate the bank approving my loan. It had bothered me more than it should have to see her talking with two guys, which is why I was awake at three in the morning reviewing security footage to see when Sarah left, and with whom. I realized I was getting into stalker territory, but I had to know. I couldn't sleep, and I couldn't risk asking Blue.

Finally, I found the time frame I was looking for. It didn't show me the table where she had been sitting, but it showed me the entry and exit points of the restaurant, inside and out. Sarah, Penn, Blue and Eryn all left together. No surfer dudes in sight. Now that I could breathe again, I needed to get a grip on myself. Why was it important to me if Sarah had a boyfriend or not, or even a causal relationship? I had them, well, not lately. But I'd had plenty of them until.... until I met Sarah. That had to be a coincidence.

I needed to grab a couple of hours of sleep before heading back to the restaurant.

At noon I got a text from Blue, "Do you have time to golf this weekend?"

"Sunday."

"Pick you up at seven."

I pocketed my phone. Golf might help loosen me up a bit. Now that I had the approval, the work was just beginning. I really needed Sarah's help to get this ball rolling. With the Seabreeze already demanding all my time, I needed help to keep this running. I needed to be able to hand some things off to someone else. Sarah was the best candidate I could think of. The problem was, even if she were willing to join the team, it wouldn't be until April after the wedding, which was only three weeks. I suppose I could manage it if she would help me part time. I pulled my phone back out of my pocket and texted Sarah. "Hi, can we get together and chat?"

I waited a few minutes before I received a reply.

"Yes, when?"

"Tonight?"

"I'm free tonight."

"Do you mind if we meet away from the restaurant?"

It was several minutes before she replied, and I thought she might say no.

"That is fine, directions?"

I realized I was holding my breath. I sent her my address.

"See you around, seven?" She asked.

Seven must be my lucky number today.

"Seven is good." It really wasn't. I had hoped she might meet me later, but I would make it work.

I left the restaurant early. I needed to shower and change before Sarah came over. I knew the staff could handle things without me, but I made them promise to call me if anything crazy happened just the same.

I had a chicken marinating in the fridge and planned to cook it for Sarah.

It was just a few minutes past seven when the doorbell rang. I was ready, but a thrill of excitement flamed up in my chest like a bonfire. What was that about? It wasn't like this was a date, and certainly not the first time Sarah and I had spent time together. I needed to calm down, or she was going to bolt.

I opened the door, and she stood there smiling nervously. But she was gorgeous. Her hair was down, and she was wearing a pair of black denim jeans and a gold top that set off the natural highlights in her hair.

"Hello, I'm glad you came."

"Hi."

I realized I was blocking the door, so I stepped aside. "Please come in."

"Thank you."

She stepped just inside the door, enough for me to close it.

"How was work today?" She asked.

"Ah, well, we were a little busy." My mouth was suddenly dry, and I couldn't think of anything else to say.

"But you left early?" She looked at me, puzzled.

"Well, yeah. I wanted to talk to you." Bringing over a glass of white wine, I explained. "I didn't have time the other night, things were so.... busy."

"Yeah, that was quite a crowd. Is it like that every year?"

"It is always a popular night, but this year was bigger than last year."

"What did you want to talk about?"

"I had hoped we could celebrate, and I could thank you." I tried to sound relaxed.

"You got the loan already?" She asked with surprise and excitement in her voice.

"I heard from the bank before St. Patrick's Day, and I invited you all there because I wanted to celebrate the good news with my friends."

"Oh, Chuck that is wonderful!"

She jumped up out of the chair and hugged me. It was quick and innocent, and it burned the heat of her body into mine. I hugged her back and felt the blood draining from my head.

I released her and took a step away.

She lifted her wineglass. "A toast to your success."

I reached for my glass. "To you. I couldn't have done it without your help."

We both sipped the wine.

"So, what's your next step?" She asked, sitting the glass down on the table.

"For starters, I made dinner as a sort of thank you for your help."

"Really?"

"Why do you look so surprised?"

"No man has ever made dinner for me before."

"What do you mean? I've cooked for you at the restaurant," I argued.

"Sure, but that is at the restaurant, you're cooking anyway. This is," she paused, "more personal."

I wanted to tell her that yes; it was personal and even at the restaurant it was personal because food is how I show people I care about them. But I didn't want to risk making her uncomfortable, so I held my tongue for once. I tried to change the subject.

"Do you like chicken?"

"Yes, I do." She smiled.

"Wonderful, I hope you like this."

I could feel her eyes on me as I moved around the kitchen. It wasn't an uncomfortable feeling, but it was making my mind go to places it shouldn't, not yet.

"So, did I hear correctly? You took up surfing?"

She laughed lightheartedly, "I've been once with Eryn recently."

"How did you like it?"

"It was scary and fun at the same time. Do you surf?"

"A little, but not in a very long time." I took the chicken out of the oven.

"Do you need some help with any of that?"

"No, I've got it. What prompted you and Eryn to go surfing?"

"Well, it was a hectic day at work, and we were both suffering from the stress of it, so Eryn decided we would spend the rest of the day at the beach."

"Must be nice to have a boss who can declare it a surf holiday." I laughed.

"I seriously doubt that will be a habit. It shocked me that Eryn even suggested she leave work early. She is too much of a workaholic normally for something like that."

"I got that impression from Blue." I plated the food while we talked.

"Really, Blue said she was a workaholic?"

"Well, maybe not his exact words, but on nights when Blue isn't working, and Eryn is, he normally stops by the restaurant for a beer or two."

"Blue seems like he might be the workaholic type, too."

"Oh, trust me he is." I nodded and brought the plates to the table. Sarah smiled, "This smells wonderful."

"I hope it tastes the same."

"Oh, I'm sure it will."

I picked up my fork and waited for her. "Go ahead, try it."

I watched as she closed her eyes and chewed.

"Hmm, this chicken practically melts in your mouth. The spices are delicious!"

I waited until she was finished with dinner, and I broached the subject of my job offer.

"Sarah, I have to ask. Have you considered my offer?"

"I have been giving it some serious thought lately." She nodded.

"And?"

She took the last bite of chicken and pushed the plate to the side. "I am going to be honest with you."

I leaned back. A lead up like this couldn't be good. But I tried to remain neutral.

"I am very intrigued by the idea of learning the food industry." She laughed nervously. "I even stopped by the library and checked out a bunch of books on the subject."

I remained quiet and let her continue.

"And while I want to do more than just be the bookkeeper and office manager at the garden center, I don't want to be just the bookkeeper and the office manager for a restaurant either. I want more. I want to contribute more."

She leaned back and sighed, like she had been waiting to tell me that for quite some time.

I thought to myself, is that all? I can handle that. But I wanted to be respectful, and this was something that clearly meant a lot to her, I wanted to help as much as I could.

I leaned forward on the table. "Is furthering your education part of your over-all plan for the future?" I asked.

She looked at me in surprise showing on her face.

"Yes."

I nodded. "Okay, I see. Then I have to revise my offer."

She sat up straight in her chair; her shoulders were tense; her gaze was laser focused. I could tell she was nervous, and I wished I could help her understand she didn't need to be this uptight around me. Maybe that was something she would learn in time. She lifted her chin a little, and all I could think about was how determined and fierce she was and how I wanted to protect her.

"I would like to re-offer you the position to be my business manager on the condition that you go back to school and get your degree. You will work regular hours but, also, we will make sure you have enough time for class, homework, and proper sleep. Any deviation from this work schedule will have to be approved by me."

Her jaw went slack, and she blinked. I watched as she processed the information. I knew she was expecting me to say something completely different.

"I'm sorry?" She asked.

"I would like to offer you the job, but I also want you to get your degree. I want you to pursue your career wherever that takes you and I hope that at least for a time that is with me. Sarah, you are so smart, and you don't even realize it. Things that come so easy to you most people struggle just to understand. And you are kind, you care about people, your friends, your co-workers. I really need you as part of my team if I have a chance of being successful. I can't do it all alone, and I don't want to do it with anyone else."

I watched while she opened and closed her mouth with no sound.

"Sarah? Are you okay?"

"I.... I don't know." She finally stammered.

"Can I get you some water?"

"No, I'm fine. More wine?"

I poured another glass. She gave me a small smile of thanks and took a sip, then closed her eyes for a moment and seemed to find herself again.

"I honestly, don't know what to say."

"Say, yes."

A broad smile spread slowly across her face. "Yes."

Now it was my turn to stare at her in disbelief. "Yes? Really?" I asked.

She nodded. "Yes."

"Here's to new beginnings." I held up my wineglass.

"To new beginnings."

"This calls for a special celebration and I have just the thing." I got up and cleared the plates.

"Here, let me help." She offered.

"Absolutely, not! I have been experimenting with a new dessert and I believe I finally have it right. Will you do me the honor of being the first person to taste it?" I asked, bringing the dish to the table and setting it down in front of her.

"Yes, of course."

"Great...," I prepared to set a plate in front of her.

"Wait, unless it has coconut in it."

"What?" I looked at her, confused.

"Does the dessert you created have coconut in it?"

"No," I drawled.

"Okay, then I will try it."

I relaxed a bit. "You don't like coconut?"

"Despise it."

"Really?"

"Yes, is that a problem?"

"No, it's not a problem. I've never met anyone who didn't like coconut before. Is it just shredded coconut or anything coconut?"

"Any and everything. Not especially that nasty little stale tasting shredded coconut flakes they used to ruin an otherwise perfectly wonderful chocolate cake," and she held up her hand for emphasis "no coconut oil for cooking. None of it!"

"Whoa! Okay. So, no German Chocolate cake, coconut pie, pineapple coconut upside down cake."

"Or coconut shrimp."

I put a hand over his heart, "That one hurts."

She laughed. "Especially coconut cookies." She declared.

"That is quite a list, but I think I've got it."

"This dish involves honey and chocolate, are those okay"

"Yes." She nodded her approval.

"Thank goodness. I was about to have a career change."

We both laughed so hard. Tears were running down her cheeks. I'm sure it was partly from the stress relief of discussing the job.

"This is the most incredible thing I've ever eaten." She looked up from her plate. "I'm not kidding, I don't want to eat anything else ever again." She took another bite.

"I'm glad you liked it," I said, clearing away the dishes once again. "More wine?"

"No, please, I'll need a cab to get home if I drink anymore."

"How about I make some coffee and we relax for a bit before you have to drive."

She hesitated, but then the wine started talking.

"That would be lovely."

I made a pot of coffee and settled Sarah in on the sofa. I could see she was a little too tipsy to drive, and I didn't want to take chances. If she had refused the coffee, then I would have driven her home by myself. But I was glad she wanted to stay.

"Here you go." I sat down next to her, leaving a space in between us.

She took a sip of her coffee and I involuntarily thought about how cute her lips were puckered up on the rim of the coffee cup. She looked me in the eye when she caught me staring. I smiled, not knowing what else to do. A stray lock of hair fell across her face, and I had the urge to reach out and brush it to the side for her. But she just left it there, letting it shield her left eye.

"So, what are you going to do next?" She asked.

I cleared my throat. "What do you mean?"

"You have the loan, what's your next step?"

For a moment I wondered if she had read my mind. I was relieved when I realized she was talking about the business and not all the things I was thinking about we could do on this sofa instead of drinking coffee.

"Well, to be honest, I really need someone to help me with the financial side of it. I need to research purchasing additional equipment. The food truck, staffing, marketing," I paused, "There are a million things to do."

Sarah watched me intently while I talked, then studied her coffee for a few minutes.

"I'm looking forward to doing this with you. I can't guarantee I will want to do it forever; I dream of having my own firm with a staff to help people and small businesses."

"I'm excited, too! You can't appreciate what a relief it is to know that I will have some help moving forward. And I understand about not wanting to leave Eryn right now. So, I'll work around your schedule."

It was the least I could do. I really wanted Sarah to come work with me. I had every confidence she could handle it, and I enjoyed spending time with her. I knew we would work well together.

She smiled. "I have to admit, I'm pretty excited and terrified all at the same time."

"Why terrified?"

"Because I'm worried, I won't live up to your exceptions. That I will be more of a hinderance than a help."

"We are both learning this as we go. We'll learn together."

"Yes, but you have to admit you have one heck of a head start in this business."

"We all have to start somewhere. Don't worry about it." I reached out and touched her hand. She looked down but didn't pull away. I let my hand linger, then dragged it away. I felt like things could take a turn in that moment and as much as I wouldn't mind allowing it to go down a more romantic path, I feared it might derail the relationship before it ever really had a chance to get started.

"More coffee?" I asked, standing up.

"Um, no I should probably be going."

Sarah stood up as well, still holding the coffee cup.

"Here, let me take that." I took the cup and placed it on the coffee table. "I'll wash it later." I walked her to the door.

"Thank you for dinner," she said, turning to face me.

I've never wanted to kiss a woman more than I did at that moment. She was so close, her eyes hooded, her lips soft and pink, and I was anticipating just how they would taste.

"Text me when you get home, so I know you are safe. Okay?"

"Sure," she nodded. "Thank you again, the dinner and the dessert were wonderful."

"Anytime." I smiled, praying she would leave, because it was getting really hard to control my urge to kiss her.

She smiled and turned away. I watched her get in the car and drive off, taking a little piece of my heart with her. But she had finally agreed to come work with me. I smiled, knowing this was only the beginning.

Chapter 16
Chuck

"Hey Chuck," Blue greeted me as he walked past the hostess stand on the way to the bar.

"Blue, what are you doing here on a Friday night, why aren't you out with Eryn?" I was headed back to the kitchen after checking on a few of the guests.

"Because she is working, again."

"She is the only person who works harder than you do." I laughed.

"She says it is just until after the wedding," Blue frowned as Brandon, the bartender, slid him his beer.

"Well, if makes you feel any better, I asked to see Sarah tomorrow, and she said she had to work too."

"Yeah, thanks to you hiring her, Eryn works twice as hard."

"So, this is my fault?"

Blue sighed, "No man, it's not. I am just eager to get the wedding done with."

"Well, are you sure much will change after you get back, I mean Eryn works hard, I don't see her stopping soon."

"She will have less pressure after the wedding. I'm sure knowing you are going to be gone for two weeks is making her crazy. She's never taken that much time off from work before."

"Sarah will still be there then."

"Yeah, that is the only reason she even agreed to go on a honeymoon for that long."

I laughed and shook my head. "Well, you know how she is going to feel when you get those phone calls in the middle of the night and have to go into the office."

Blue just stared at me and took a pull from his beer.

"Okay, okay." I held up my hands in mock surrender. "I'm going back to the kitchen. You enjoy your beer."

"See ya." Blue grumbled. I had learned long ago it was best to leave him alone when he got into one of these moods.

Saturday afternoon, Sarah arrived at the restaurant wearing jeans and a black t-shirt. I couldn't take my eyes off of her. How was it possible she looked even more beautiful in jeans than in a sexy dress?

"Hey, good to see you." I greeted her as she poked her head into the kitchen.

"Hi, is this a good time?"

"Of course." I washed my hands, took off my toque, and followed her to my office.

"Wow, you've been doing a little spring cleaning, I see." She looked around the tiny office.

"Well, I want this to be your office." I said, looking around, noticing there was still much to be done.

"What? No, where will you work?"

"I work in the kitchen most of the time anyway and the stuff I do in here, is what you'll be doing so can have the office. It'll be fine. I just need to get a few more things out of your way."

"Chuck, I really wasn't expecting this." She protested.

"Did you expect I was going to make you sit in a corner somewhere?" I laughed at her expression. "Trust me, this is for the best."

I sat down in a guest chair, showing she should sit behind the desk. I watched her as she reluctantly sat in my old chair. "We can order you a better chair."

"No need. This one will be fine. We need to keep costs down or at least confined to the food truck related expenses."

I smiled. Sarah was determined, and I could see she had a bit of a stubborn streak in her. I liked it.

"Okay, no chair. How long will it take to get a food truck operational? I mean the warm weather is practically here and I'm afraid we will miss out on the wedding season this year, but can we get something together for mid to late summer?"

"Okay, let me look at the numbers." She said, opening her laptop. "We need to decide first what we are going to serve on the truck, obviously not the full menu. So where do you plan to focus your attention?"

I could see she had already been working on this, and it impressed me.

"You're right, it can't be the full menu and it needs to be something people can handle easily on a paper plate, so I was thinking Po'boy sandwiches, perhaps seafood tacos, stuff like that." Truth was, she had clearly put more thought into this than I had.

"Okay, let me do a little market research and see who else is serving that sort of food. We want to make sure we stand out. Do you have a portable signature dish?"

"Uh, not really." I admitted.

"Okay, you may want to reconsider that one, something you might want to be known for. Do you plan to serve alcohol from the food truck? Because that will be an additional license we need to get."

"No, I hadn't planned on serving alcohol, but we will need one for the catering business for larger events where truck might not be appropriate for formal weddings and stuff."

She nodded while she tapped on the keyboard.

"Also, I printed off some materials from a couple of different colleges. I wanted to get your opinion on the programs they offer."

I sat back in the chair. "Okay, what did you have in mind?"

"Well," she began pulling papers from her bag, "Batten has everything I need, a master's program in business. They also have a hospitality program. And there are some online schools as well."

She looked up to make sure I was following along.

"What do you think?" I asked her.

"Well, Batten University being local has its advantages, but the in-person classes they require are during the day which could create interference with the work schedule. The other schools are one hundred percent online, but they cost more."

I held up my hands. "Okay, let's get to the important part of selecting the school, take the work schedule and the cost out of the equations. Which one do you want to go to? Which one has the program to suit your overall career goals the best?"

Sarah looked at me for a moment, "Okay, I see what you are saying, but...,"

"Sarah, there are no buts. You will have plenty of opportunity to work late into the night, so day classes are not a problem. We have a tuition assistance program here, so again cost is not the issue. The only thing that matters is which school do you want to go to?" I waited for her to answer.

"Are you familiar with Batten's hospitality program?"

"I am."

"What is your professional opinion of the school and the programs? Would you give someone preference when hiring them based on the Batten program versus another school?"

"I would, but you're not going just for the hospitality program you need to determine if the MBA program is worthy of your time as well."

She looked at the documents and then up at me. Her expression conveyed her bewilderment. I understood choosing a school was an overwhelming experience, and I was grateful I would never have to do it again.

"You don't have to decide today which school. I'm just telling you when you weigh your options, don't let the work schedule or the cost prevent you from choosing a school you really want to go to. Pick the best program for you, the rest we can work out."

She nodded, "Okay. Thank you." She scooped the papers back up and returned them to her bag. She looked a little disappointed.

"What's wrong?" I asked.

"Nothing, I just need to do a little more research."

"Okay, that's fair."

She sat there for a minute chewing thumb nail, which meant she had something on her mind.

"If you have something you want to ask, Sarah, just ask."

"Where did you go to school?"

"Batten."

"Really?"

"Yes." I laughed. "Why does that matter?"

"Because, you then have a realistic opinion about the school and it's programs and whether your experience was good or bad is at least based on experience."

"True. Talk to some of the other staff members and ask about their experience as well."

"Thank you. I will do that." She tapped on her laptop some more. "I have made a list of the licenses and permits that are required to operate a food truck in Gates Point and the surrounding cities and counties. I'm sure you are probably already aware of most of these since you have the restaurant, but I made a list just the same. It also helps me."

I nodded, "I'll let you take the lead with that sort of thing."

She nodded and made some notes.

"Have you researched what kind of truck you want to have, the size, or if you prefer a trailer that will need to be pulled?"

"I'm glad you asked. I have been thinking about that weighing the pros and cons to both and I've made a list of possibilities and the costs associated with them."

She gave me a look that said she was surprised I had done the work and then she smiled, a genuine smile, the kind that made her eyes crinkle in the corners. The kind of smile I wanted to see every day for the rest of my life.

"I'll email it to you and we can go over it together." I said, pulling out my phone and sending her the document.

"Got it." She said, more tapping. "Do you want to come around here so we can see it on a larger screen?" She asked, rotating the laptop and moving her chair so we could share the screen.

I shifted the metal guest chair over to the corner of the desk.

I pointed to the screen. "This one is my first choice; it can fit everything we need, and it's pretty mobile, it isn't too large and can almost fit in a normal parking space. The drawback is storage capacity."

She nodded and followed along.

"Now this one over here." I paused and looked at her hand on the external mouse for a moment. "Do you mind, it might be easier?"

"By all means." She moved her hand away, but not before mine was already reaching for the mouse, and my hand briefly covered hers. Heat shot through my body like a lightning bolt. Sarah put her hand in her lap quickly. If she felt the same flash of heat, she didn't show it. She politely avoided eye contact and concentrated on the screen. I completely lost my train of thought.

"Um, this one." I fumbled with the mouse and click on another tab on the spreadsheet. "No, that's not it."

I could see a hint of pink in her cheeks as I tried to regain my composure. What was wrong with me? Women didn't make me lose the ability to speak. I wasn't a Casanova, but I was normally in more control than I was at the moment. I pulled it together and showed her two other options I had included.

"Chef, we need you." Todd called from just outside the door.

"Be right there."

"Excuse me but stay as long as you like to work. Let me know if you need anything you can't find in the office."

"Thanks." Sarah nodded, but her attention was already drawn back to her laptop. *Eryn has been a bad influence on this girl if she wasn't a workaholic before.*

Chapter 17
Sarah

"I accepted Chuck's offer." I announced to the girls as we sat in Penn's office drinking wine after work the following Tuesday.

Eryn and Penn both stared at me.

Penn sat her wine glass down slowly. "When did this happen?"

"At dinner, the other night."

"Dinner? You didn't tell me you were having dinner with him." Penn looked offended.

"Shut up Penn and let her talk." Eryn said, still clutching her glass.

"He invited me over for a celebratory dinner because he got the loan for the expansion. We started talking about next steps, and I said I'd come work for him." I bit my lip and looked at Eryn.

"That is wonderful! Congratulations!" Eryn leaned over and hugged me.

"Are you sure?" I said, still feeling like I was abandoning my friend.

"I am sure! You need to follow your dreams, your passions. No one ever stopped Penn or I."

Penn sat, looking a little sour.

Eryn turned to Penn. "Aren't you happy for Sarah?"

"Of course, I am, but what does this mean for us?"

Eryn looked at her puzzled. "What do you mean, us?"

"Well, she is going to be too busy for us now," Penn looked as if she might cry, "and I love having you around."

"Penn, I'll have time for us, we will still do things together, I'm not moving away." I tried to smile, but she had a point. I would be working long hours at least in the beginning, and I wasn't sure if Chuck expected me to work at the restaurant when he did and that wasn't exactly nine to five. So, my social life was going to take a hit.

Penn pouted a little, "I'm happy for you but I'll be completely sad if we don't still go to dinners and," Penn paused staring off into space for a moment, "Does this mean you won't be able to model for me anymore?"

I swear I thought she was going to get the vapors.

Eryn rolled her eyes, and I stifled a giggle.

Eryn scolded her. "Penn, get a grip and stop thinking about yourself for once."

Penn frowned, "Fine, but you have to understand the things we do have a ripple effect throughout our little group." Penn was staring at Eryn, and I got the feeling this was rooted in Eryn's upcoming wedding and had very little to do with me and my new job.

I reassured Eryn I wouldn't leave the nursery until after she returned from her honeymoon, but that meant I began the search for my replacement. I wanted to get someone in as soon as possible to give me enough time to train them leaving Eryn and the business in excellent hands. I contacted a few people from my old firm, plus posted an ad online. At Chuck's request, I started looking into degree program requirements, schedules, and cost. I printed off information from Batten University and a couple of on-line schools to decide which was a better fit for me. Batten had a few online classes, and they were the only local college with a hospitality program. I had decided to pursue a joint master's in business administration and hospitality. It was just that the in-person classes were in the middle of the day, and that might be a problem with the work schedule with Chuck. I wanted to discuss it with him before making a final decision. Batten was also less expensive than the online schools, and since Chuck was going to be paying for most of it, I needed to be careful about how much I was spending.

It was finally Friday afternoon, and I was looking forward to the weekend, even though I planned to work Saturday morning on reviewing the applications I had received so far for my replacement. My phone buzzed with a text from Chuck.

"Do you want to get together tomorrow morning?"

"Can't, working. Tomorrow afternoon?"

"Afternoon is good. Meet me at the restaurant?"

"Sure."

The butterflies in my stomach fluttered the way they did every time I was around Chuck. Now that was extending to text messages and phone calls. I needed to get them under control. I wasn't sure how this was going to work, being so attracted to him and working together, but my desire to learn more and gain more experience outweighed my attraction to Chuck. Relationships were temporary. My career would be for the rest of my life, and I would not let a man interfere with my long-term goals.

By the time I got home from the garden center, I was exhausted. I grabbed a microwave dinner and ate it in front of the TV. I had to admit, I was excited to work at the restaurant the next day. There was so much to learn and so much to do. Chuck had been kind enough to give up his office. Working so close to the kitchen, I spent half the day listening to all the banter and conversations as the team prepared the food. I woke up at two in the morning in front of the T.V. I stumbled to bed knowing I would be tired when the alarm went off.

It was a struggle to get up to go to work, but it was my own fault. I ran the shower colder than normal to help clear the cobwebs out of my head, then I made coffee to go. On the weekends I wore jeans, so I didn't have to worry about what to wear today. Jeans and a sweater should be fine for both jobs.

I didn't get to the garden center until nine o'clock. Eryn was already in the retail greenhouse arranging trays of seedlings.

I waved as I headed inside from the parking lot.

I refreshed my coffee and then plopped down at my desk to begin the bittersweet task of reviewing the applications for my replacement.

It was a little surreal and the first three I set aside as not acceptable. I hoped there would be at least one suitable candidate in the stack of twenty.

"Hey there, you've been at it a while, want to take a break?"

I looked up to see Eryn standing in my doorway.

"I'm almost done for today." I leaned back. "I can't look at anymore."

"Want me to take a look at them?"

"I don't want to burden you with this, you've got so much else on your plate."

"Like what? You and Penn have the wedding under control. I can look at them after you've weeded out the ones you think need to be passed over."

"Okay if, you're sure." I handed her a folder with six applications in it. "I won't tell you, my preferences. You look, and we can see if we have the same thoughts."

"Sounds good. Do you have plans this afternoon?"

"Yeah, I'm going over the Seabreeze when I leave here."

Eryn looked concerned. "Make sure you aren't working too hard."

I laughed, "Looks whose talking!" I turned off my computer.

I was up early and back at the restaurant on Sunday morning. Chuck had given me a key, so I let myself in and settled into the office to work. I had been working for about an hour when Chuck came in.

"Whoa! Sarah, you scared the hell out of me." Chuck stood gripping the door frame.

"Sorry, I'll get out of your way. I just wanted to get an early start."

"No need to apologize, I'm just not used to anyone getting here before me."

"I'll go work at one of the tables while you have your quiet time in the kitchen." I closed my laptop and started to leave.

"No, no, please. Don't leave."

I slowly sank back into the chair. Chuck smiled. "I'll stay out of your way. Have you had breakfast?"

"Uh, well, no. But you don't need to cook for me."

"You can't do your best without a nutritious breakfast. What did you have for dinner last night?"

"Uh,"

"It must not have been very good if you don't have a response." Chuck offered with a grin.

"It was Salisbury steak, at least I think that is what it was supposed to be, anyway. You can never really be sure with those frozen meals."

"Again, with the frozen meals, haven't we been down this road?" Chuck looked horrified.

"Uh, well, I'm not a skilled cook, and I was exhausted when I got home. I wasn't really in the mood to go to a lot of trouble."

"Sit, please do not tell me anymore. My heart can't take it."

Chuck began gathering up ingredients. It was all very magical, the way he moved around the kitchen, grabbing this and that and making it all come together. He presented me with eggs Benedict and fresh fruit, with freshly squeezed orange juice.

"This is so beautiful. I can't eat this; it is a work of art."

"Thank you." Chuck gave me a small bow. "But the better compliment would be to enjoy it."

I smiled and picked up my fork. "As you wish." When I was done, some of the other staff members had arrived, and the kitchen was getting busy for Sunday brunch. Chuck replaced my empty plate and juice glass with a cup of coffee.

"Now, you may return to work."

It was a polite way of shooing me out of the kitchen so they could all work, but I didn't mind.

Several hours passed unnoticed until a member of the kitchen staff, whose name I learned was Robin, appeared at the doorway to the office.

"Excuse me, Sarah?"

"Yes?" I looked up, and she was holding a plate.

"Chuck sends this with a message."

I sat back in my chair. "What is the message?"

"He said to tell you to take a break and eat something healthy."

"Oh, that is very nice, but I brought my lunch." I pulled out a burrito wrapped in foil from the convenience store I passed on the way to work.

Robin rushed in and snatched the burrito from me.

"You can never let Chuck see you bring something like this in here, ever!" She whispered.

She put the plate on my desk. "Please eat that or he will have my head." She turned on her heel and I heard the thud of my burrito hitting the garbage can.

I stared down at the southwest chicken salad and decided I might as well eat it, since my burrito was no longer an option. It was certainly cold, anyway I had picked it up off the roller at about seven this morning.

Having finished the salad, I pushed the plate aside, and returned to work. I was doing a little market research on the food trucks in the area. I was sure Chuck had his own ideas about what to serve, but I wanted to help him finalize his decision.

There was a knock on the door. "You are doing, okay?" Chuck asked.

"I'm fine. Maybe later, we can talk about a few things?"

"Yeah, absolutely, as soon as the rush is over, that okay?"

"Of course, whenever you're available." I smiled.

But it was a busy Sunday, and the rush was not over. I had plans to meet Penn for dinner.

I packed up my bag and looked for Chuck in the kitchen. He was supervising the cooks, so I waved, "Chuck, I have to go." I shouted over the din.

He looked up and waved and returned his attention back to the cooks.

I met Penn at the Yacht Club downtown.

"There you are," Penn waved. "Good lord, you look awful."

"Gee, thanks."

"I was just about to go get a massage; I'll see if Alan can fit you in."

"Penn, you don't need to do that."

"I don't need it, but you do."

She grabbed me by the arm and dragged me along to the spa. I tried not to notice as people turned to stare as we walked by, me in tow, like a petulant child.

"Maggie, dear, can you see if Alan has time for my friend Sarah here?" She pushed me forward as if I were on display. The receptionist looked up and gave me a sympathetic smile. "I'm sure we can find someone to help you."

After a moment of typing on the computer, Maggie assured me that Gina could help me, and Penn led me back to the locker room. I changed into an incredibly soft robe and slippers and followed Penn to the waiting area, which was equipped with a juice bar, pitchers of ice water and a bowl of fresh fruit. There were several other ladies waiting, either watching the muted TV or reading a magazine.

"Penn, I've never had a massage before. What do I do?"

"And it shows, honey." She patted my arm. "Just relax, Gina is great, and she will take good care of you."

"Sarah?" A woman wearing scrubs in the club's colors appeared in the doorway.

"That's me." I said nervously.

"Right this way." She gave me a warm smile. "Is this your first time?"

"Yes, ma'am." I said, following her into a private room.

"Okay, well, we have different options available; you can get a massage just to relax or if you have tense muscles from sports, I can offer you a deep tissue massage."

"I don't play sports. My favorite pastime these days is stress." I tried to joke.

Gina put on some relaxing music. "What kind of stress?"

"Well, I'm currently working two jobs and helping plan a friend's wedding."

"You aren't kidding when you say stress, are you? Okay, we are definitely going to need to get you in a more relaxed state. Here, take a whiff of each of these oils and tell me which one you like that best." She said, picking up two dark brown bottles from the table.

She handed me the bottles separately.

"The second one."

"Wonderful choice. Okay, now you can take off your robe." She held up a light sheet and turned her head to give me privacy. "Then you can hop up on the table face down."

I did as instructed, and she laid the sheet over me. I wasn't sure what I had expected, but I was relieved to learn that so far, the experience was more dignified than I had imagined.

She began working the oil into my skin and massaging my shoulders. "So where do you work?"

"At the moment I work full time at Sandcastle Garden Center and part time at the Seabreeze."

"You must work for Chuck."

"Yes, that's right. You know him?" I asked cautiously.

"He and I went on a couple of dates. Chuck knows how to have fun."

My shoulders tensed up and hoped that Gina didn't notice.

"I'm sure he does."

"I don't mean that in a bad way. He likes to do fun things, but he isn't the serious relationship type." She paused. "I'm sorry, are you guys dating?"

"No, not at all. I'm the business manager."

"If you're ever bored on the weekend, just give Chuck a call. He is good for a movie or a ride in the country on that big Harley."

"Thanks, I'll remember that." Suddenly the allure of the massage had been lost. I don't know why. It was none of my business how Chuck spent his free time. It surprised me he had time to date anyone based on his work habits.

She continued the massage in silence, and when she was done, Gina offered me a bottle of water. "I'll give a few minutes of privacy, there's no rush, enjoy the feeling and the music."

I was up off the table as soon as the door shut. I had my robe on and was headed out with my water when I nearly knocked Gina down coming through the door.

"Oh hey, I hope you feel better." Gina smiled.

"I do! Thank you, that is just what I needed." I found Penn in the waiting area.

"There you are. God wasn't that wonderful?" She sighed.

"Yeah, is there a place I can shower and get this oil off of me?"

"Uh sure, right through here." Penn led me back to the locker room. "Just over there."

"Thanks!"

I showered and got dressed.

Penn eyed me, but she didn't ask questions.

"You want to have dinner?"

"I'm not very hungry, but I wouldn't refuse a glass of wine."

"Fair enough." Penn led the way to the bar. We found a table and ordered a bottle of wine.

"I don't believe I have ever seen anyone come out of a massage more tense than before they went in. You don't look like that massage helped you at all, sweetie." Penn fussed.

I glared at Penn for a moment and sipped more wine. "I have no idea what you are talking about."

Penn laughed. "Well, I know that is bullshit. So, what happened?"

"Nothing happened. Gina is just a little too chatty; it was hard to relax with her talking the whole time."

Penn mumbled something into her wineglass. Then asked, "Are you sure you don't want something to eat?"

"Why does everyone keep trying to feed me?" I snapped. "But please order something if you like, don't let me stop you."

Penn ordered a shrimp salad. I poured more wine.

"Your stress level has nothing to do with your new job, does it?" Penn asked between bites.

"No, the job is exciting." I meant it.

"Okay. You want another bottle of wine?"

"Yes, definitely."

"You are planning to work at the nursery tomorrow, right?" Penn asked.

"Of course, why wouldn't I?"

"Because I'm just wondering if you will be able to get up in the morning after drinking this wine."

"I'll be fine." The fact that after two bottles I thought I would be fine should have been a clue that I was already not fine.

"Come on, I'll give you a ride home." Penn said.

"Okay. But what about my car?" I giggled.

"We'll worry about it tomorrow." Penn put a sympathetic arm around my shoulder, and we walked to her car. "Just one thing," Penn said as she slid behind the wheel.

"What's that?"

"Do not under any circumstances throw up in this car."

I laughed. "That's silly." I put my head back on the buttery soft leather and closed my eyes for a few minutes.

There must not have been any traffic because it seemed like I had just closed my eyes and we were at my apartment.

"Come on, sleeping beauty." Penn said, putting an arm around me and helping me out of the car.

I could hear voices around me in the distance. Maybe someone was having a party.

Then I felt weightless. "Good night, Penn."

"Good night."

I heard a soft laugh. But the blankets were tucked up under my chin and they felt so good. I let myself drift off to sleep.

Chapter 18
Sarah

My alarm buzzed way too early and entirely too loudly. I slammed my hand down on the clock. But the beeping continued. I fumbled to find my cell phone and stop the noise. My head was pounding, and my mouth felt like I'd been chewing on cotton.

I groaned and rolled out of bed. I was wearing a t-shirt and my panties. I didn't remember changing my clothes. I stumbled to the kitchen to make coffee; I stopped and leaned against the refrigerator to let the coolness seep into my head. While I was standing there, I inhaled the scent of coffee. My mind must be playing tricks on me I thought. Perhaps Penn had set up the coffeemaker last night. Bless her if she had.

With one eye open, I rummaged through the cabinet, looking for my favorite mug, it was missing. I looked in the sink and it wasn't there either. Perfect. At this moment it didn't matter, I just needed coffee.

"Looking for this?" Chuck's voice said from behind.

I gasped and spun around. He was standing there smiling, holding my coffee mug.

"Here." He smiled and handed it to me.

I should have been scared, or mad, but what I was, was desperate for coffee; I wordlessly took the mug and sipped. I closed my eyes and let those magical coffee beans do their thing. I kept my eyes closed and took another sip. The human part of me was reemerging.

Then I remembered I was wearing only a t-shirt and panties. I kept my eyes closed trying to determine if I was just having a weird wine induced dream. I opened one eye. Nope. Chuck was standing there grinning at me.

"Oh. My. God."

"Morning."

"What are you doing here?"

"Well, that is kind of a long story. It might be best if we can talk about it after you get dressed." He continued to watch me.

I looked down and screamed. I ran to the bedroom, spilling coffee along the way. I locked myself in the bathroom and looked in the mirror. Big mistake.

I jumped in the shower without waiting for the water to get hot. The blast of cold water sobered up me faster than the coffee. I took extra time drying my hair and brushing my teeth before dressing and returning to the kitchen.

Chuck had helped himself to coffee and was leaning against the counter drinking it when I returned.

"Good morning." He lifted the coffee cup in my direction.

"Good morning, did you make the coffee?"

"I did."

"Thank you." I poured myself another cup. "I don't want to sound rude, but what are you doing here?"

He smiled. "Well yesterday at work you wanted to talk but I got so busy we never had the chance. So, after work I stopped by, but I found Penn trying to extract you from her car and she looked like she needed a little help."

"I see. That was last night. Did you leave and come back?"

"No, I never left." He smiled a thoroughly wicked smile. "You probably don't remember. But I held your hair while you threw up about one o'clock this morning."

"Oh god," My cheeks burned in embarrassment. "I think I am completely mortified." I sank to the kitchen floor.

"Hey," Chuck sat down beside me. "What are friends for?"

"This is the most embarrassing thing I have ever done."

"Really?" Chuck looked amused. "Well, you have led a very sheltered life."

"I just don't even know what to say." It was clear he wasn't going to leave and spare me the indignity of coming to terms with my behavior last night, but I guess here on my kitchen floor was better than confronting it at the restaurant.

"You must have a pretty awful opinion of me right now."

"Why?"

"Coming home drunk, not even remembering any of it."

"I'm sure you had an excellent reason because you are not a party girl."

"Why do you say that?"

"Because a party girl wouldn't have thrown up after just four glasses of wine."

I stared up at the ceiling, this wasn't getting any better.

"Hey, Sarah. Don't sweat it. We've all had days or nights that we need to just do something we don't normally do. I just hope working for me wasn't the cause of this."

What was I supposed to say? I wasn't even sure why I did it.

"No, I had some things bottled up and I guess they just came out."

"That's understandable."

"Come on, I'll give you a ride to work." He stood up and offered me his hand and helped me off the floor.

"So do you want to talk on the way to work?" Chuck asked.

"We can, and I'll have to email you later what I found, but I was doing some market research of the type of food trucks in the area that might help you decide what you wanted to specialize in."

"Thank you, that was very thoughtful. Based on your research, do you have a recommendation?"

"Well, I would suggest doing something a little more high-end. There already seems to be plenty of sandwiches, soup, hotdog, pizza, burger, and snack trucks out there. If your goal is larger crowds, you may want to try something unique. I don't think anyone is featuring a farm-to-table truck or wild game. I read about a truck that only serves alligator."

He looked at me for a long moment and I feared I had overstepped.

"Thank you so much for doing all of this, I've had some ideas, but you were smart to do the market research first."

I nodded, not really knowing what else to say.

"I mean it, this is exactly why I wanted to hire you." He smiled.

"Well, I'll email you all of this. I should get to work."

It was his turn to nod. "Talk later?"

"Yeah, sure." I opened the car door and slid out. "Thank you for the ride."

"Anytime."

I walked straight to my office, hoping to avoid any awkward questions. But my luck doesn't run that way.

Eryn popped her head in my office. "Hey are you feeling, okay?"

I thought Penn must have told her.

"Yeah, I took something for the headache and already had a cup of coffee. I'll live."

"It would have been okay if you called out sick."

"What? No way, not over something stupid as a hangover."

"Wanna talk about it?"

"What did Penn say?"

"Just that you guys had dinner at the club, and you drank yours."

I sighed and rolled my eyes to the ceiling.

Eryn came in and sat down. "This must be bad."

"It is the worst of the worst."

"Okay, start at the beginning."

"Let me just start by saying I realize it is stupid."

"Okay, so noted."

"It was a great day at work with Chuck. I mean, I didn't really see him that much. But he gave me his office which was totally unnecessary, and I spent my time working and doing my thing while he did his thing out there in the kitchen."

Eryn nodded.

"Then I met Penn, and she said I looked stressed from working two jobs and I needed a massage. So, I agreed."

"And...."

"And I've never had a massage before, so I'm lying there naked in front of a total stranger, and she is making small talk. So, I tell her where I work, and she tells me how she used to date Chuck and how Chuck is always up for a good time and whatever."

"Okay, well, I bet you sort of realized that already."

"I did, sort of. And this is the stupid part. Why do I even care? It is totally none of my business. But I don't know why I got aggravated and started drinking and the more I drank the madder I got."

"Sounds like you were mad at yourself."

"Yes, I was. Because I was mad that it bothered me, that she dated Chuck or that Chuck dates a lot and is not really into commitment. I mean why?" I raised my face to the ceiling, "Why do I even care? This makes no sense."

The corner of Eryn's mouth twitched a little, "Because maybe you do care, and you don't want to admit it."

"Well, even if that were true, and I'm not saying that it is, any chance of having Chuck interested in me is completely blown."

"Why?"

"Because, apparently," I paused, trying to maintain my composure, "he was at my apartment last night when Penn brought me home. He came by to talk about work stuff and helped Penn get me inside. And here is the very best part. He stayed the night and held my hair while I vomited!" I covered my face with my hands. "I mean, I don't even remember any of it and then he made me coffee. I'm not even sure if he or Penn undressed me, but it doesn't matter because when I woke up this morning in a t-shirt and panties, which by the way, he saw me in."

"Well, you're gorgeous so I don't see the problem."

"The problem is, I don't know him well enough for him to see me half naked but then after someone holds your hair while you puke, I guess not much else matters."

Eryn laughed.

"I really don't consider it that funny. I have to quit my job at the Seabreeze now."

Eryn stopped laughing. "For god's sake, why?"

"Do you really expect me to work with him after this?"

"Why not, if you are not attracted to him and he is just a friend? How is it any different from working with me or Penn?"

Damn, she was good, and she had me cornered. I either had to admit that it wasn't any different and I would have to show my face in the restaurant, or I admit I was attracted to Chuck, and I wasn't prepared to admit that at the moment.

I stared at her. She smiled back at me, knowing full well what she had just done.

"Fine, he's cute."

"Cute, hell he is smoking hot and cooks too? Are you kidding me? Blue is lucky I met him first."

"Eryn!"

"I'm just saying." She waived her hand in the air.

"Well, I don't see there is anything to worry about. By all accounts, he just likes to have a good time and isn't into anything serious. And while I don't need a relationship right now, I'm not into the 'for a good time call', scenario either."

Eryn laughed lightly, "Okay, well I'll give you a ride to your car after work tonight."

"Okay, thanks."

Eryn left me alone with my thoughts, which was a dangerous thing to do under the circumstances.

I didn't even look up from my computer until lunch time when Eryn popped her head in my office again.

"Excuse me, Sarah. You have a couple of visitors." She gave me a wicked smile and left before I could ask questions, Chuck's face replaced Eryn's.

"Hey there, I hope I'm not imposing."

I stood up, "Not at all, please come in." I wondered what the hell he was doing here.

Chuck stepped into my office, followed by Ray, who worked in the kitchen.

"Ray and I brought your car to you and some lunch." Chuck held up a bag.

Great, now Ray realized what a loser I was, too.

"Oh, uh, thanks. You didn't have to do that. Eryn was going to take me after work to retrieve my car."

"That is okay, Ray and I are out doing some shopping for the restaurant, so it was on our way."

I glanced over at Ray, who smiled sweetly and nodded. Somehow it made me feel a little better.

"Well, we can't stay. I just didn't want you eating something from the microwave today. You need something in your stomach."

I winced at the memory of last night.

"Why do you assume I packed a frozen lunch?"

"I saw your fridge and freezer. They are deplorable and I found a very offensive burrito in the trash can at work."

"You rummaged through the garbage?"

"No, I didn't go through the garbage, but I smelled something god awful in it and I noticed the roller food wrapper when I was taking it outside." He winked at me.

Ray was making motions behind Chuck that showed I shouldn't argue.

I remembered what Eryn had said earlier about Chuck being good looking, and I refocused my attention from myself and my humiliation to admire how good-looking Chuck was standing there in my office in jeans and a t-shirt.

"Thank you."

He gave me a genuine smile. "You're very welcome."

"Here are your keys." Ray said, handing them over.

"Thank you. You saved me a lot of time."

"Well, we have to run, drink lots of water today. It will help."

"I'll do that."

Chuck turned to leave; Ray was trailing behind him. He leaned back and whispered. "He must really like you."

"Ray, let's go!" Chuck called.

"Coming, Chef." Ray strode away.

I smiled as I stared at the white bag on my desk.

Chapter 19

Sarah

"You can come in now, Eryn." I called out after Chuck and Ray left.

"Did you call me?"

"You heard me." I laughed.

"So, what did Chuck have to say."

"He was kind enough to bring me my car, so you won't have to take me after work."

"Wow, that was really nice of him."

"And he brought me lunch, want to share?"

"You bet!" Eryn sat down.

"Chuck apparently has a problem with my menu choices for lunch."

Eryn laughed. "I bet he does."

I peeked in the bag and found two large boxes and two smaller ones.

I put the bag on the floor and the boxes on the desk, "Let's see what the chef has prepared for us."

"For you, I'm just mooching." Eryn opened one box while I opened the other.

"What do you have?" I asked.

"A delicious looking salad, fruit and chicken breast."

"I have fruit, a cookie and fish. Want to split it?"

"Yes! I'll get silverware." Eryn jumped up and ran to the kitchen.

We split the cookie and the fish and chicken.

We ate in relative silence. The food was delicious and exactly what I needed.

"Wow, that was good. I swear Sarah, you better hold on to that man."

"He isn't mine to hold on to."

"I bet you could change that with very little effort."

"Let's see what is for dessert." I said, attempting to avoid talking about my feelings for Chuck.

"Ooh," Eryn grinned as she opened the container.

I opened mine. "I have some sort of chocolate cake."

"I have cheesecake."

"Oh, I've had his cheesecake, and it is fantastic, you'll like it. Want part of my cake?"

"No, that's okay." Eryn eyed the cheesecake.

Who could blame her? We each ate our dessert, enjoying every morsel.

"Oh my god, I think I'm in love!" Eryn sat back in the guest chair.

"Hopefully, with me!" Blue said, leaning against the doorframe of my office.

"I don't know, is it possible I could love two men at the same time?" Eryn said, not at all deterred in her admiration.

"Depends on the other man."

"Chuck." Eryn smiled up at Blue.

"Absolutely not! I will not share you with Chuck Thomas."

"Fine, but you're going to have to learn to make cheesecake." Eryn stood up to kiss Blue on the cheek.

"On second thought, it might be easier just to let Chuck have you on the weekends." Blue laughed.

I admired the way they bantered playfully with one another. Each secure in their relationship and their place in it. There was no jealousy, no spite. They were a walking advertisement for genuine love.

"So, what prompted this sudden infatuation with Chuck?" Blue looked from Eryn to me.

"Oh, Chuck was kind enough to bring Sarah lunch, and she shared it with me."

"Really? Wow, I didn't know Chuck delivered."

Eryn tossed me a secret smile. "Yes, well, apparently it is an employee benefit." Eryn ushered Blue away from my office.

I cleared up the empty boxes and pulled out my phone to send Chuck a text.

'Thank you for lunch.'

"It was dinner too, but I suspect you shared it with Eryn."

"I did."

"I can deliver dinner later if you like."

"Thank you, I'll be fine."

"Not if you plan on eating what you have in your fridge."

"I'll go to the store," I lied.

"Okay. Gotta run."

I slipped my phone back into my pocket and got back to work, finalizing my decision on my replacement by checking a few references before I shared my choice with Eryn. Doubt was creeping in; I was having second thoughts about leaving here, but I had made a commitment to myself to improve my skills and create a career. I needed to do this. Truthfully, there was no way I could afford college without Chuck's help, so this was a smart move.

I didn't see Eryn again until it was time to go home, and she stopped in.

"Sarah, go home. Get some rest."

"I'm fine. I'll go soon. I just have a few things to finish up."

"Like what?"

"It can wait until tomorrow, but I am wrapping up reference checks on my replacement."

"Oh." Eryn's expression told me she wasn't happy I was leaving either.

"I don't have to go." I blurted.

"Sure, you do. Chuck is a great guy, and it is a great opportunity. Besides, if it doesn't work out, I'll have Blue kick his ass and you can come back here."

"I could work for you on the weekends and Chuck during the week?"

"And when would you have time for school and sleep? This is the smart move, and we'll stay in touch. We will still have girls' nights, and Penn really likes you. She will not let you go."

"Really?"

"Sure, I've been trying to get rid of her for years and you see how well that has gone."

"You lie; you two are like sisters."

Eryn laughed. "That's true. Come on, this can wait until tomorrow, go home."

"Okay." I turned off my computer and packed everything up. Once in my car I realized how tired as I was, and I really didn't want to go home. I wasn't sure what I wanted to do. But sitting home alone wasn't it. Calling Penn was out because the idea of reliving the details of the night before or a bunch of questions about what happened after she left me in Chuck's care was not something I wanted to experience. I was tempted to go to the Seabreeze, but I decided that seemed too clingy since Chuck had brought me my car and lunch. Finally, after driving around for an hour I just went home. I looked in my fridge and then the freezer. Chuck was right. This situation was pathetic. Just a week ago, I would have been perfectly happy with a frozen meal and a romantic comedy, but now I wanted more. I wanted something I could actually taste and a serious romantic movie with genuine feelings. The movie I could find; the food was a problem. I settled for something in a box that was called gourmet and it was anything but. I zapped it in the microwave and sat down in front of the TV and was disappointed in the movie and the food. I tossed the uneaten portion and showered and went to bed. I wasn't in the mood to sleep on the sofa tonight, either. What had gotten into me?

I managed to get through the rest of the week without embarrassing myself any further. I made an offer to my replacement and set a start date.

Friday afternoon, my phone buzzed with a text from Chuck.

"Hey why don't you come in tomorrow afternoon and work later."

"Okay?"

"I was thinking you could get some experience in the front of the house for a change."

"Yeah, cool!"

"See you around noon."

I immediately made plans to sleep in and have a proper breakfast before going in. I also didn't have plans for tonight. Which was odd since I hadn't heard from Penn today?

"Hi Sarah."

"Oh hey, Eryn."

"What are you doing this weekend?"

"Working, but not going in until noon tomorrow."

"Want to go surfing after work tonight?"

"It's Friday night. You and Blue aren't doing something fun?"

"No, he has a work thing."

"Okay, should we invite Penn?"

Eryn laughed. "No, she doesn't surf anymore besides I'm pretty sure she has a new boyfriend."

"Ah, that explains it."

"Radio silence?" Eryn asked, knowing that Penn forgets about her girlfriends at the beginning of each new relationship.

"Yeah, haven't heard from her since Wednesday. Who is she dating now?"

Eryn shook her head. "I have no idea."

I smiled. "Yeah, let's go surfing tonight. Maybe I'll do better this time."

"Even if you just lay on the board, it will be fun. I'll pick you up."

I was excited and rushed home from work to change and wait for Eryn. I never dreamed I would be a surfer. But this was really fun. I could understand why Eryn spent her youth on the water.

Eryn pulled up to the curb, boards on the roof of her Volkswagen, and I jumped in.

"Ready?"

"Can't wait!" I laughed. Eryn blasted beach music as we drove over to Virginia Beach.

"There's a storm coming in tomorrow. So, we might get some bigger waves today."

"Really?" I was excited but bigger waves made me nervous.

"You'll be fine."

We pulled on our wetsuits and waxed the boards before hitting the water.

The days had been slowly warming up, but the water was still cold by my standards, which was anything cooler than bathwater. Eryn was completely unfazed and dove right into the first wave and popped out the other side.

I paddled to keep up. My arms were going to be sore tomorrow.

We were the only people in the water, and we surfed until it got too dark.

We stumbled up the beach laughing and exhausted. I heard a rumble and looked up, hoping it wasn't thunder. But it was a group of motorcycles pulling away from the parking area. I wondered for a moment if one of them might be Chuck. But it was Friday night, and the restaurant would be busy. He wouldn't be out riding his Harley.

"Everything okay?" Eryn asked.

"Oh, yeah."

"Clouds are rolling in early; we better get back to the car."

I carried the board and followed Eryn. What was wrong with me, and why had I thought of Chuck when I heard the motorcycles? This was getting really dangerous.

Once back in her car, I leaned my head back. "I'm going to sleep like a baby tonight."

"Me too."

The next day I woke with a few sore muscles but feeling relaxed and ready to learn something new about the restaurant business. The first part of the evening I reviewed some numbers Chuck had left me about the food truck he had decided on, and the menu he was considering with supplier details. I wanted to compare his numbers with other options to see if there was a way to save some money, especially in the beginning until the truck started paying for itself.

"Hey there, you ready for your dinner break?"

I looked up, and Chuck was standing in the doorway holding a plate.

"Oh, I don't even know what time it is, I guess so."

"Good, put the computer away, enough number crunching."

I laughed and did as he requested.

"Tonight, ma'am, we have a duck with roasted potatoes and a salad."

"There is no way I should eat this much food. Please tell me you are going to split this with me."

"That is all for you, made this evening by the skilled hand of chef in training Ray."

"Really? Well, I'm sure it will be delicious."

"Mind if I join you?"

"Please and get silverware, because honestly, I cannot eat all of this. Are these the portions you give your customers?"

"Does your brain ever stop worrying about the numbers?"

"Sorry, occupational hazard." I gave him a sheepish grin. The aroma was wonderful, and my stomach growled, reminding me I hadn't eaten since ten o'clock this morning.

I savored the duck; it was incredible. I only remember having duck one time before, and it wasn't as good as this.

I ate until I was full and still had half of it left.

"Are you done?" Chuck looked concerned.

"I swear I can't eat another bite."

"What about dessert?"

"You seriously have to stop feeding me like this or I'm going to gain too much weight."

Chuck picked up my fork, picking at what was left of my dinner. I watched him, amused that it was natural to him that he was so comfortable in our relationship that he didn't mind eating off my plate. I hadn't stopped to consider if our relationship was more than just business, because I had been trying so hard to keep my feelings in check that I hadn't realized we had become friends as easily as Eryn, Penn and I had.

"Did you go out with the girl's last night?" Chuck asked between bites of roasted potato.

"Just with Eryn. Penn has a new boyfriend, so we won't see her until the shine wears off of that one." I laughed.

Chuck shook his head.

"What?" I got defensive over Penn.

"I don't understand people who have those types of relationships."

"What do you mean?"

"Men and women who date so casually and by date, I mean have intimate relationships. And then in a few weeks or even a couple of months have moved on."

I sat back and crossed my arms, the words of the massage therapist, Gina, ringing in my ears.

Now it was Chuck who got defensive.

"What?" He put the fork down.

"That sounds a little hypocritical to judge Penn that way."

"Hypocritical? Why would you call me a hypocrite?"

"Because you do the same thing."

"What! Who told you that?"

"Gina, the massage therapist, I met last weekend."

Chuck blinked at me.

"You remember the pretty girl that works at the yacht club?"

"She told you she and I had an intimate relationship?"

I wanted to say yes, but then realized that she never actually said they were intimate.

"She said you were always ready for a good time."

"And you think 'a good time' is sleeping around?"

"No, I don't."

"So, did she give you any examples?"

"Well, I don't remember exactly." I was suddenly feeling idiotic. "What about that girl who used to work here and had to quit because her car broke down?" I tried again.

"She was an employee, and I gave her a ride home twice. She is a big fan of Harleys. And I'll admit she is a bit of a flirt, and we went to a couple of local music festivals, but there was no 'dating' and there certainly wasn't any kind of romantic relationship."

Suddenly I was very ashamed of myself. And I realized I might have really offended Chuck, but he looked at me and a funny lopsided grin spread across his face.

"What?" I asked.

Chuck leaned in and whispered, "so you met Gina last Sunday at the yacht club with Penn?"

"Yes, that's right." I nodded, not really seeing the point to his question.

"And after you had your massage, you and Penn had dinner?"

"Yes."

"And you got drunk."

My face burning with embarrassment. He had figured it out.

"You could say that."

"I do say that. I was there for the aftereffects, and you were bombed."

He was practically laughing at me. "What is your point?"

"Did you get drunk because you assumed I was dating Gina or a bunch of girls?"

"Why do you think my getting drunk had anything to do with you?"

Chuck wasn't even trying to hide his amusement at this point. "Because your face is bright red, and it tells me the truth your lips won't tell."

"Well, that is completely ridiculous!" I said, fidgeting with the stapler and pens on my desk.

"Uh huh, sure. Then why did you get drunk?"

"Who says I need a reason!" I sounded like a five-year-old even to myself.

Chuck stood up with a hearty laugh. "Shall I take this away for you, ma'am?"

"Yes, please!" I reached for my laptop, not knowing what else to do. I had been caught red-faced and there was no getting out of it.

I stood up and walked into the kitchen, needing some fresh air. There were a couple of people working, Chuck was nowhere to be seen. Ray was grabbing something from the cooler as I walked past on my way to the back door.

"Ray, thank you for dinner. It was the best I've ever had."

"You're welcome." Ray beamed.

I stepped outside into the night air; it was not too warm, not too chilly, probably around fifty-eight degrees. I could see the stars and I scanned the sky for the Big Dipper. I inhaled deeply. The air was a mix of salt water and food from the restaurant.

I heard the door open behind me, but I didn't turn to see who it was.

"It's a nice night, isn't it?" Chuck whispered.

"Yeah." I kept my eyes towards the sky, and I was grateful it was dark. I side stepped into the shadows a little more so he wouldn't be able to see my cheeks blush.

"Listen, I'm sorry about earlier. I didn't intend to embarrass you and I'm an ass."

I dropped my gaze, but still couldn't bring myself to look him in the eye.

"I don't think you're an ass."

"Well, I acted like one, and I didn't mean to. I'm really very sorry."

"Thank you." My voice was weak, and I hoped he couldn't tell that this made me blush even more than his teasing. "It's okay. I shouldn't have been embarrassed. Once you've seen a girl puke, all bets are off." I tried to laugh a little.

"What's a little hangover between friends?" Chuck leaned over and bumped me gently with his arm.

"You're right, that pretty much breaks all the boundaries." I laughed out loud.

"Want to learn about bartending?"

"Sure!"

"Come on." Chuck held the door for me as we went back inside.

Chapter 20

Chuck

I felt bad about teasing Sarah, she had been so embarrassed. It had started as a joke, but I quickly realized that it wasn't a joke to her and although we were maintaining a professional relationship that maybe she had feelings for me as well. Mine had only grown stronger for her after spending the night nursing her through her first-time binge drinking.

When I returned to the office to apologize to her, she was gone. I panicked, fearing she had left, but her laptop was still on the desk.

"Anyone see where Sarah went?"

"Outside for some fresh air, Chef." Ray pointed to the back door.

"Thanks, man."

Sarah was just outside the back door in the shadows, staring at the sky. I needed to apologize, and prayed she'd forgive me, and for some strange reason, she did. I wanted to make amends, so we walked up front to the bar.

"Martha, have you met Sarah, our business manager yet."

Martha was my lead bartender and soon to become bar manager. She had worked for me for three years and was amazing; she knew every drink you could imagine, she was great with the customers, and she didn't take any crap off the drunks.

"Nice to meet you." Martha held out her hand.

"Sarah is a walking computer when it comes to numbers, and she is eager to learn the business. You can help her with that, right?"

Martha smiled. "Of course."

I left Sarah in Martha's capable hands and headed to the dining room to check on the guests before heading back to the kitchen.

I checked on Sarah around ten o'clock and the bar was busy, even for a Saturday night. She seemed to handle things, and Martha was using her as the bar back while she and Brandon poured the drinks.

After last call, Sarah helped Brandon and Martha clean up. I left them to it.

Thirty minutes later, the silent alarm was triggered and came up on my phone. I carefully looked out towards the bar to see a man pointing a gun at Martha and Sarah. I backed into the kitchen and ducked out the back door, making my way around the front. I slowly crept up the stairs to the front entrance and silently stepped inside. I could hear the man's voice. Fear for Sarah bloomed in my gut. I had to get to her; I had to keep her safe.

"I said put the money in the bag!"

"And I said I have already deposited the money. There is nothing here to give you!" Martha yelled back.

"Prove it! Open the register!"

"Listen, she told you..." Brandon tried to argue.

I knew the money was still up there and I appreciated my employees' loyalty, but we were going to have a serious talk about safety after this.

"Then give me your tips; I know you didn't deposit those."

I stalked the guy and slowly crept up behind him. Sarah was laser focused on the gun, and I doubt she could see anything else. She looked terrified. Brandon saw me and stalled the guy. He patted his pockets like he couldn't remember where he put the cash.

"Hurry! You too, honey." The man said to Sarah.

"I don't......" Her voice trembled.

"She is in training; it's her first night, and she doesn't earn tips yet."

"Fine, whatever, just hand it over!"

I was close now; I nodded to Brandon. Making my move, I grabbed the guy's gun hand by the wrist and twisted it around. Brandon pushed Martha and Sarah to the floor in case the gun fired accidentally. As the would-be robber and I crashed to the floor, the police charged in and surrounded us.

"Police! Don't move!"

I let go of the guy and put my hands out to my side.

The robber was on his knees, still holding the gun.

"Drop the gun, do it now!" The police ordered again.

For a minute I didn't think the guy was going to drop the gun. I was concerned if the police shot him and missed, a bullet might go through the bar and hit Brandon, Martha, or Sarah.

Finally, he complied, and the gun hit the floor with a thud. The police handcuffed me and the suspect until they could get things sorted out. Martha, Sarah, and Brandon stood up and were immediately surrounded by uniformed police.

"Chuck, are you okay?" Sarah called out.

"I'm fine," I said as an officer helped me to my feet. "Everything is going to be okay." I tried to reassure her. She still had that wild-eyed look of fear, and I wished I could go to her. I wanted to wrap my arms around her and tell her everything would be alright.

Martha put her arm around her instead.

"Sir, can you tell us your name?" An officer asked.

"My name is Chuck Thomas; I'm the owner and my ID is in my wallet in my back pocket."

The officer looked at me like he wasn't sure if he trusted me or not.

"Okay, can you tell me what happened?"

"The alarm went off, and I came up front to investigate. I saw this man holding a gun on my employees, so I jumped him."

"That wasn't the smartest idea."

"Maybe not, but it worked. He didn't shoot anyone, and he was still here when you guys got here."

The officer frowned. He removed the wallet from my pocket and verified my ID. He removed the handcuffs and handed me my wallet.

Sarah, Martha, and Brandon were each being interviewed by the police while two more officers escorted the robber to a police car.

One officer snapped to attention. "Evening Chief." I pulled my eyes away from Sarah to see Blue walking through the front door.

"Chuck, is everyone alright?" Blue asked, as he shook my hand.

"Yeah, physically, we are all okay. They are shaken up." I nodded to the trio at the bar.

"Sarah is having a tough year." Blue said, looking her way.

"Why do you say that?"

"Earlier this year she had a stalker that was really harassing her."

"He the one that kidnapped Eryn?"

"Yeah, that's the one."

"Poor kid."

"Chief."

Another officer walked by, Blue nodded.

"I guess it's a big deal when the chief comes out." I said.

"I heard it on the radio, thought I'd come check on you."

"Thanks."

"Anything stolen?"

"No, the staff stalled him long enough for me to take him down."

"Glad to see all that training came in handy." Blue laughed.

"Semper Fi. I need to go check on...,"

Blue nodded. "Go on."

As I approached, the uniformed officers were finishing up and walking away.

"You guys, okay?"

"I'm okay, good timing Chef, thank you." Brandon nodded.

I gave him a nod then turned to Martha and Sarah, "What about you two?"

Martha still had her arm around Sarah.

"We could use a minute."

"Go back to the office, it's quiet in there." I watched as Martha led Sarah away. I poured her a shot of whisky.

"She looked pretty shook up." Brandon observed.

"Yeah, having a gun pointed at you is pretty scary."

"Yeah." Brandon nodded. "I'll see you tomorrow."

"Take the day if you need it, no harm."

"I'm good."

I walked to the office carrying the glass of whisky. I figured Martha was probably okay; she was pretty tough and had been in the business a while. Sarah, on the other hand, was probably a little more disoriented by the experience.

I knocked on the door, then opened it slowly. Martha was kneeling in front of Sarah, who was crying.

"Can I come in?"

"Sure," Martha stood up. "Sarah, I'm gonna go now."

"Yes, thank you. I'm sorry you had to see me like this." Sarah apologized.

"Don't worry about it, sweetie, it's going to be okay." Martha patted her arm and left.

I put my hand on her back. "Hey there."

She looked up at me. "Hey." Her voice barely above a whisper.

"What can I do for you?" I asked.

"I don't know."

She shook her head, and I could see she was fighting back more tears.

"Drink this, it will steady your nerves." I held the whiskey towards her.

"No, I don't want a drink." She tried to push it away.

"It's medicinal, it's okay."

She smiled and took it.

"Down in one." I instructed.

She did as she was told and immediately began coughing and sputtering. I put my arm around her and patted her back gently. "It's okay. Hang in there."

She finally came up for air. "That was awful. How is that supposed to help?"

I had to smile. "Looks like it is already."

She frowned at me.

"Come on, I'll give you a ride home."

She nodded and grabbed her things, and I walked her out to my car.

"No motorcycle tonight?" She asked.

"Not tonight." I opened the door for her and waited until she slid inside.

She was silent during the trip to her apartment. I didn't want to push her. I pulled up to the curb and put the car in park.

"Want me to walk you to the door?"

She sat staring out the window for a long time, and I wondered if she had heard me.

"Sarah?"

She pulled her eyes away from the window and looked at me.

"I don't want to go in there." She said. She looked frightened somehow.

"Okay, you don't have to go inside." I wasn't sure what to do or say.

Finally, she looked over at me. "I know this sounds like I'm some sort of loser, but I really can't be alone tonight. I don't want to impose on you; I'll call Penn or Eryn to see if they will let me stay with them.

"Do you need me to go inside and get you a few things?" I offered.

"No, but would it be too much to ask if you went inside with me while I pack a bag?"

"Not at all." I got out and opened the door for her and put my arm around her. We walked inside and I stood in the living room.

"I'll just be a minute."

"No problem. Take your time." I said, glancing around the room.

Sarah emerged from her bedroom, holding her phone. "Penn's not answering. Big surprise."

I reached over and gently took her phone and put it in my pocket.

"Sarah, why don't you come stay with me tonight. I have a spare room where you will be safe, and I will let you have your space."

She looked at me like she wanted to say yes.

"I'll be a perfect gentleman, I promise."

She laughed a little. "I never thought you would be anything else. Yes, thank you."

I nodded and took her bag from her and led her back out to my car.

Chapter 21

Sarah

We drove in silence to Chuck's house, I was a mix of emotions ranging from scared, to embarrassment to nervousness over agreeing to stay at his house.

"You have a lovely home." Nothing about it screamed bachelor looking for a good time.

"Thank you. Make yourself comfortable." He pointed to the living room with leather furniture and a sleek flatscreen TV mounted on the wall.

I sat down while Chuck disappeared for a moment. I was having serious second thoughts about this decision.

"How about some tea?" Chuck came back carrying a cup on a saucer.

"That sounds wonderful."

"I added a little honey. I hope that is okay. Taste it and tell me if you need anything else."

I took a sip. "This is perfect."

Chuck sat down in a chair opposite from me, leaving plenty of space between us, just as he promised. The problem was, I wished he were sitting closer. I wanted him to come over and wrap his arms around me and tell me everything was going to be okay. But how do I tell him that? He had promised to be a gentleman; I needed to be a lady and keep my promise to myself about keeping this relationship professional.

"Are you hungry?" Chuck asked after several minutes.

I laughed. "No."

"What's funny?"

"You are always trying to feed me."

"I consider food to be a way to show people you care about them."

"I'm sorry, I didn't mean any offense by it." I was embarrassed, again. He had saved me from a gunman; opened his home to me and given me a ride.

"It's okay, many people don't appreciate the importance of sharing a meal or the history behind it."

I sipped more tea, trying to hide my face.

"You're right, sharing a meal that you have prepared is important." I admitted.

Chuck smiled and watched me. "So do you know how to cook?"

"I do, I mean the basics. It just never seemed worth the time and effort for just one person. It's easier to microwave something and then I guess I just got into the habit of doing it every day."

He nodded that he understood. "I get it. I wasn't always into cooking. Of course, in the Corps you eat what they give you, so you don't have a lot of choice in the matter."

"Was the food that bad?"

"It wasn't always bad, and it depended on where we were and under what conditions. But it is hard to get specialized when you're cooking for hundreds of people at a time." He smiled.

"I would imagine so."

"I like to make each dish special. Especially, if it is a friend. I try to prepare each dish according to what they like and don't like, to tailor the meal to their personal tastes."

"I imagine that is pretty hard to do in a restaurant."

"It is, you still have more control than cooking for troops, and I have a few regulars that like a little more of one spice over another, so I try to accommodate that without them knowing."

"You're a really good-hearted man." I blurted out. It was true, but I don't know why I was compelled to say it at that moment.

He smiled. "I try."

I finished my tea and stood up.

Chuck stood up, too. "I can take that."

"I can at least wash it. You don't have to wait on me hand and foot."

"Yes, I do." He reached over and took the cup and saucer.

I followed him to the kitchen. I was feeling relaxed and, even a little sleepy.

The shock of the robbery was wearing off, and my body was feeling heavy.

When Chuck turned around from the sink to face me, I noticed how stunning his eyes were.

"Thank you." I whispered.

"You're welcome." He glanced back at the sink.

"Not for the tea."

"Oh?"

I took a step forward and was a little unsteady for a moment as Chuck reached out and put his hands on my shoulders to steady me.

"You, okay?"

"I'm fine, thanks to you. You saved us from that gunman."

"Well, Brandon and Martha should have just given him the money. I'm going to have a talk with them about that tomorrow."

"But he could have shot them even if they gave him the money."

"That is true, but unlikely. Usually, people just want the money and will leave once they get what they want."

"But you weren't willing to take that chance, were you?" I pressed.

"No, I wasn't." He admitted.

"I was so afraid."

"I'm sure you were, and I will do everything in my power to make sure that never happens again."

I noticed the heat rolling off his body, and it was hard for me not to reach out and touch him. I looked up into his eyes.

"I wasn't afraid for me."

"You weren't afraid?"

"I was afraid you would get hurt when you jumped that man. It terrified me he was going to shoot you."

Chuck looked at me in disbelief, and then he smiled warmly and wrapped me in a hug, pulling me close.

"Oh Sarah, you don't have to worry about me."

"But I was." I said against his chest. I stepped back enough to look up at him again.

"I wasn't scared until I saw you grab him. Then my heart stopped."

He blinked, and I realized he was going to lean in and kiss me, and I was going to let him. But he recovered and stepped back.

"You should probably get some sleep. I'll show you to your room."

I was disappointed that he was keeping his promise to be a gentleman. I followed him upstairs and into the guest room. It was neat, if sparse. My bag was sitting on the bed.

"I'm just down the hall if you need anything. I'll be downstairs for a while. So, you'll have some peace."

"Thank you."

"Bathroom is right next door."

He smiled and left me to my nightly rituals before going to bed. I slipped into the bathroom and washed my face and brushed my teeth and hair, then returned to the bedroom and changed into sleeping shorts and a t-shirt. My phone buzzed and there was a text from Eryn.

"I just heard, are you okay?"

"I'm fine."

"Do you want me to come stay with you?"

"No, I'm at Chuck's."

"What?"

"I just couldn't stay in my apartment alone."

"Why didn't you call me?"

"I was going to, but Chuck invited me here before I could."

"Is staying there a good idea?"

"Probably not. But I'm upstairs in the guest room and he is downstairs being a perfect gentleman."

"If you need to take time off from work, you take it."

"Why does this stuff keep happening to me?"

"I don't know,"

"Me either."

"Okay, talk to you tomorrow."

"Okay." I put the phone down and crawled into bed. I plugged in the charger and set the alarm. At least tomorrow was Sunday, and hopefully Chuck didn't get up too early. Between the chamomile tea and the whiskey, I was ready to go to sleep.

I forced myself to go downstairs and pour a drink to steady my own nerves. Sarah had talked about being afraid for me when I jumped the robber. But I didn't tell her the reason I did it was to save her. Once I saw the gun pointed in her direction, the only thing I could focus on was taking down the gunman. I stopped carrying a gun when I left the Marine Corps., I'd seen enough killing in my lifetime and it was a good thing because deep down if I had a gun with me tonight, I would have shot that man. Taking a deep breath, my hands were shaking. I also had just come very close to breaking my promise. Sarah was so close, and the physical contact was more than I could bear. I wanted to kiss her mouth so badly that I had to put some distance between us, or I would prove her right about being a player. I threw back the whiskey and waited for the burn, closing my eyes, letting it radiate throughout my body. What had I been thinking? Under what circumstances was it a good idea to have Sarah sleep under the same roof? This was going to be a long, rough night. The best thing for me to do is to stay downstairs and sleep on the sofa, if I could sleep at all. I laid back and closed my eyes. Images of the gun pointed at Sarah and the others filled my head. I squeezed my eyes shut to force the image out of my mind. But it was replaced with the man's face close to mine as we struggled, and I pinned his gun hand to his side and forced him towards the floor. The images swirled in my head and got mixed up with images of Sarah sitting behind the desk in my office. The look of fear in her eyes. Then images of Sarah in some place dark where I couldn't find her screaming for help. I woke with a start, my heart racing when I realized the screaming wasn't a dream. I raced up the stairs and burst into the guest room. Sarah sat up with a start, staring at me in the dim light.

"Sarah!"

I rushed over and kneeled next to the bed and wrapped my arms around her. She was trembling so hard her teeth were chattering.

"Shhh, it's okay. You had a nightmare. Everything is okay. You're safe."

I crawled onto the bed next to her and continued to hold her. She looked around the room wildly.

"I'm here, I've got you. We are both okay." Her body was still tense, so I reached over and turned on the small bedside lamp.

"Look at me, honey." I leaned away. "It's me, Chuck. Everything is okay, it was just a bad dream."

Her eyes began to focus, "Chuck?"

"Yeah, it's me."

"Oh, Chuck." She cried and clung to my chest. "Please don't leave me. I don't want to be alone. I'm scared he'll come back."

"I won't leave, I promise. I'll stay right here and protect you. No one is going to hurt you. I swear it."

She laid her head on my chest, and I enjoyed it way too much. It was good to have her leaning on me. Her hands clinging to me and me guarding the door for her. It was way too easy to love Sarah. She could have my heart in her hand by morning and there would be nothing I could do about it. Nothing I wanted to do about it.

I woke up the next morning with my head on Chuck's t-shirt clad chest. I had the vague memory of waking up from a dream and Chuck coming in to save me. It was all a jumbled mess in the pre-coffee fog. When I stirred, he rubbed small circles on my back.

"Shh, go back to sleep. I've got you." He whispered.

"It's okay, I'm awake."

Chuck moved under me. He was still on top of the covers while I was tucked snuggly underneath. I looked around the unfamiliar room. I had slept deeply with Chuck's arm around me, I wished I could sleep like that all the time.

"How are you this morning?" He asked.

"Much better thank you."

"I'll go down and start the coffee." Chuck got up and disappeared, leaving me to shower and dress.

I found him in the kitchen, standing at the sink looking out the window.

"This is a beautiful kitchen. Is this where all the magic happens? Where you create new recipes?" He turned at the sound of my voice.

"Yes, something like that. Coffee?"

"Please." He poured the coffee into a heavy white mug and handed it to me. "Help yourself to sugar and cream if you like."

I added sweetener to my coffee. "Would you like breakfast?"

"Oh, you don't have to go to all that trouble for me."

"I eat breakfast every morning. It would be nice to have company for a change." He said, opening the commercial grade refrigerator and retrieving eggs and bacon.

"Well, okay then." I sank into a chair.

Chuck smiled and began cooking.

"Can I do anything to help?"

"I've got it; I enjoy cooking for other people."

"Okay. How about I pour you more coffee?"

"Yes, thank you." I got up and filled his mug of coffee and put it on the counter near where he was working.

"Listen," I was standing on the other side of the island, "I really appreciate you letting me stay here last night. I'm sure it was an imposition."

"Not at all. The room never gets used and I'm glad you came to me for help."

"Chuck," I waited for him to look at me. "I meant it last night when I said I was afraid for you. I still am."

Chuck took the pan from the burner and set it aside.

"You never need to worry about me. I'll be fine. But I will always make sure you are safe."

I believed him; I didn't ask how he would protect me. But I also got the feeling now was not the time to ask how he planned to accomplish this. Chuck turned to the cabinets and just like that, the conversation ended. Over breakfast, I asked about Brandon and Martha.

"They are okay, sadly both of them have had a similar experience before. I'm going to make sure it doesn't happen again in my restaurant."

"Chuck you can't take that all on yourself, you can take precautions but if it is one thing I have learned, it is that you cannot control what others do."

"Do you want to talk about it?"

"I realize Eryn doesn't blame me, but I still blame myself for her being kidnapped. I still have nightmares about it."

"But the man is in jail?"

"Yes, he is in jail, and I'm sure if he ever gets out, he'll have to face Blue. He did that once; I don't think he will want to do that again."

"I'm sure not. But I'm not interested in Blue. I want you to tell me what he did to you."

"We worked for the same company. He was in IT, and I was in accounting. He seemed like a nice enough guy, a little socially awkward, but I didn't hold that against him. We had only gone on a couple of dates, and he started talking about getting married and having children and that I wouldn't have to work anymore. When I told him, I didn't want to go out with him again, he started following me and the more I rejected him the more violent he became." I shivered at the thought. Chuck stood and came around to my side of the table and kneeled in front of me.

"I'm so sorry to make you relive that. I didn't mean to make you uncomfortable." He put an arm around me, and I was in fact safe here with Chuck. Chuck nodded. "Do you want to take the day off?"

"No." I answered quickly. Again, Chuck nodded.

I didn't want to let this incident dictate how I lived my life. "Will Martha be working today?"

"Yes, she will be in around four this afternoon."

"Can I work with her again or did you want me to do something else?"

"Do you think you will feel up to working in the bar again?"

"Yes, I have a lot more to learn."

Chuck smiled, "Sure."

Chapter 22

Sarah

Sunday after work, I drove home. If I was honest, I wished I could have found another excuse to stay with Chuck. But what kind of message would I be sending, I don't like you, now I like you? Isn't there a name for that? And what proof did I have that he had feelings for me? He had been a good friend, yes. He had also been the perfect gentleman.

The next morning, Eryn and I pulled into the garden center parking lot at the same time. "Morning, Eryn."

"Morning, Sarah. Are you certain you should be at work today?"

"I'm fine. I worked at the bar again last night."

"Really, are you sure that was a good idea?"

"I can't live in fear, remember?"

Eryn looked pensive, "I know I said that about Rob, but this is a little different."

"Is it? I mean, this was random. I wasn't the target, none of us were. He just wanted money."

"Blue said Chuck took the guy down before the police arrived."

We walked into the store together. "Yeah, that was the scariest part of the whole thing."

Eryn paused at my office door. "How so?"

"It scared me when the gun was being pointed at us, and I was hoping if we just gave him the money, he would leave, and everything would be okay. But, when Chuck came up behind him and grabbed him, it terrified me the gun would go off and Chuck would get hurt."

"Yes." Eryn had a funny expression on her face. "I see what you mean."

I settled in and prepared for the new the employee to arrive. I had to get her trained enough to take over for me after the wedding. My last day was going to be on April 16th, the day Eryn returned to work from her honeymoon. I wouldn't be in the nursery that much while she was gone, probably only part time so I could spend more time at the restaurant. Hopefully, the new food truck would be delivered by then and we would stock it and get ready for events later in the spring and into the summer.

"Good morning." A voice sounded from the doorway. I looked up to see Tammi, the new hire standing there.

"Good morning, come in." I stood up to welcome her. "I apologize it is going to be a little tight in here for about a week. But you can put your purse there in the file cabinet for safekeeping."

After her things were put away, I led her into the hallway, "let me show you around again."

I had given her a tour on her second interview but, I'm sure things were overwhelming that day and it wouldn't hurt to give her another tour. We spoke to Eryn and then headed out to the retail area and the greenhouses. My phone buzzed around lunchtime with a text from Chuck.

"Just checking to make sure you are okay and eating something that didn't come out of a microwave."

I had to laugh. "Too busy for lunch today."

"Please, eat."

"I will." I lied. I would not have time to eat, not with Tammi in training and the rest of my work to do. Paychecks had to go out on Friday. Tammi was eager and caught on quick. I let her observe the payroll process, then gave her a project to work on. She had brought her laptop so she could work sitting at the table in the kitchenette. At five o'clock Tammi knocked on my door.

"I think I made excellent progress on the project today; is it okay if I leave now?"

I glanced up at the clock, "Oh my gosh, I didn't realize the time. Yes, of course." I smiled up at her. "Thank you for all your hard work today. See you tomorrow."

Tammi retrieved her purse. "See you tomorrow," she said brightly, and bounced out of the office.

I turned my attention back to my computer. A few minutes later, Eryn stuck her head in the door.

"I'll be out in the greenhouses for a while; if I don't see you before you leave, have a glorious night."

"Okay, see you tomorrow." I looked up briefly. I was eager to finish what I had started. I was almost done when my phone buzzed this time, and it was an actual phone call.

"Hello?"

"Hi, it's Chuck."

"Hi, how's your day going?" I asked, leaning back in my chair.

"Fine. How's yours?"

"A little busy, the new girl started today, and you know how that is." I laughed a little at my own joke.

"I'm going to assume then, that you did not eat lunch today."

"No, I just didn't have time."

"So, what are you having for dinner?"

"Uh, I hadn't given dinner much thought." I heard Chuck sigh into the phone.

"Well, tell me what you have, and I can tell you what to whip up."

"I'd love to but I'm still at work; I can't remember what is in the fridge."

"You're still at work? Eryn works you too hard."

"Eryn isn't even here, or if she is, she is out in the greenhouses."

"Sarah, I don't like you being in there alone, is the door locked?"

"Honestly, I'm not sure. I would assume Eryn locked them when she left the office."

"Have you finished your work for the day?"

"Yes, I was just shutting down my computer."

"Why not come by the restaurant and I'll fix you dinner."

"That is really sweet, but if I come by, I am going to work and honestly I'm tired."

"Okay, promise me you'll eat when you get home."

"I promise, leaving now." I reached down and grabbed my bag from the desk drawer.

"Can I call you later?" he asked.

I was curious at Chuck's sudden interest in my habits.

"Sure. You have a good night at work." I said as I walked to the employee's only door that led to the parking lot.

"Talk to you later."

I clicked off and walked to the car, curious but also excited by the attention from Chuck. I told myself on the drive home I needed to not get read too much into the phone call. He was probably just checking on me to make sure I didn't have some sort of post-traumatic stress after the robbery or something. He'd probably called Brandon and Martha, too. Hurrying into my apartment, locking the door behind me, I headed to the fridge. There was milk, eggs, bacon, bread, and a head of lettuce, perfect for a BLT on toast. I started the bacon and ran to the bedroom to change. I put on my, dinner in front of the TV uniform, which was soft fuzzy socks, sweatpants, and an oversized t-shirt. Then ran back to the kitchen in time to turn the bacon over. I popped the bread into the toaster and retrieved a plate from the cabinet. I wondered what wine goes with a BLT. Tonight, it was going to have to be red because it was all I had. The bacon was done, so I built my sandwich, poured the wine, and headed for the TV. I flipped through the channels until I found a movie and settled in. I fell asleep about halfway through the glass of wine. My phone buzzing on the table woke me up.

"Hello?" I answered in my best groggy voice.

"It's Chuck, were you asleep?"

"I must have dozed off after dinner." I said, sitting up straight, suddenly very much awake and alert at the sound of Chuck's voice.

"Please tell me it wasn't anything frozen."

"No, I cooked, and everything was as homemade as I could get it."

"Wow, okay I'm impressed."

"Thank you." I smiled to myself.

"I won't keep you, I'm sure you're exhausted."

"No, it's fine. How's your night going?" I stifled a yawn.

"It's a little slow," His voice trailed off.

"I'm sorry. I'm sure things will pick up."

"Oh yeah, they will. I'm not complaining as slow nights are good, they help balance the scales for the crazy busy weekends."

He had a point. Friday through Sunday in the wintertime were the busiest days. But when the warmer weather was here to stay and he could open up the deck, every night was going to be busy. People coming in from the water on their boats and even kayakers would paddle up. And on the weekends, it would be pure chaos.

"Okay, well, I'll talk to you tomorrow." Chuck said.

"Okay, good night." I padded to bed, carrying my phone with me. Tomorrow would be another day of training. The days were counting down fast to the wedding and Penn had been on complete radio silence. I was getting worried, so Tuesday morning before Tammi came, I sent her a text to make sure she was okay. It was noon before I heard from her. She came breezing into the nursery. I heard her when she came through the door and waited until she made it back to my office.

"Ah, there you are, Sarah, my one staunch friend. The only person who checks up on me to make certain I am alive."

I heard Eryn's voice, which told me she was standing in the hallway, just out of my view. "I talked to you last night, drama queen."

"Yes, but I text you first so that doesn't count."

I rolled my eyes. Tammi looked from me to Penn and back again.

"Penn, I'm glad you are here. We have a new employee I'd like you to meet." I said, introducing her to Tammi.

"Oh hello, dear." Penn looked at Tammi as if seeing her for the first time.

"Hello." Tammi smiled. Her expression was the same I'm sure I had the first time I met Penn. She is quite glamorous, and you get the impression you're in the presence of someone very famous. I stifled a giggle.

"Well, I stopped by to see if anyone would like to go to lunch."

"I'm afraid I can't. I am swamped, and it is only Tammi's second day, I don't want to leave her alone."

"Oh pish, she won't be alone, and she'll probably be glad not to have you looking over her shoulder for an hour."

Tammi looked like she wanted to disappear.

"Penn, leave them alone." Eryn scolded.

"What? I'm sure Tammi can mind the store, or you wouldn't have hired her."

Tammi looked at me and in a very low voice whispered, "It's okay if you want to go, I can shadow the retail staff."

"Are you sure?" I whispered back.

She nodded.

"Okay, Penn, where are we going?" I said, retrieving my purse.

Penn winked at Tammi. "See, she is already to go on her own," Penn turned her attention to Eryn. "You're coming too."

"I wouldn't miss it." Eryn gave Penn a forced smile.

I smiled at Tammi. "You don't have to work up front if you don't want, and feel free to call me if anything comes up."

She nodded.

"Can I bring you back something?" I offered.

"Oh, thank you, no. I brought lunch."

"You sure?" Penn asked.

"Yes, ma'am. Thank you."

The three of us walked to Penn's car.

"What did you have in mind for lunch?" Eryn asked again.

"It is such a beautiful day, let's go someplace we can sit outside. What about the Seabreeze?" Penn suggested.

Eryn frowned. "You're going to take Sarah from one job to another for lunch? Seriously?"

"It's fine." I said hoping to avoid an episode of Eryn and Penn bickering.

"See, she is okay with it."

"Penn, please can we go somewhere else?" Eryn continued.

"Why?" Penn looked at me in the rearview mirror, "Is there trouble in paradise?"

"No, it's fine."

"What am I missing here?" Penn demanded.

Eryn scolded Penn. "Sarah was nearly robbed at work this past weekend and perhaps she would not like to go back for a while."

I rolled my eyes. Sometimes I wondered why I even tried talking to either of them.

"Why am I just hearing about this now?" Penn demanded.

I leaned as forward as the seatbelt would allow. "Because it was no big deal. I wasn't robbed or shot, and I went back to work on Sunday."

"I'm sorry, Sarah." Penn was sincere.

"Can we please just go to lunch; it is no big deal."

"Do you want to go someplace else?" Eryn asked.

"No, the Seabreeze is fine. And Penn is right, it is a perfect day for sitting on the deck."

I wanted to change the subject and take the attention away from me. "How are things going with your new beau?" I asked.

Penn sighed. Eryn glanced at me over her shoulder as if to say, 'and here's the reason for the lunch visit.' I suspected as much. Penn was bored with her latest boyfriend, or they had already broken up.

"He is fine, he is off on some business trip this week."

"Oh, a career man?" Eryn asked. I could hear the amusement in her voice.

"Yes, he is the CEO of a marketing firm."

Eryn couldn't control herself any longer and laughed out loud, "So not some poor little boy toy?"

"No."

"He has his own career and responsibilities?"

"Yes."

I snickered in the backseat.

"I'm glad you find this amusing." Penn sniped.

"So, he finds time to dote on you anyway?" Eryn continued.

Penn sighed dramatically, "not as much as I would like."

By the time we arrived at the restaurant, Eryn, and I both were crying with peals of laughter. We walked up to the hostess stand.

"Three for lunch?"

"Yes, and may we sit on the deck?"

"I'll have to see if we have anyone assigned to that area." The hostess looked up and saw me standing there.

"Oh hi, Sarah. You guys can go right on out, if you like."

"Thanks, but don't go to any trouble for us." I offered.

"It's no trouble, I'll send someone out to you."

Penn looked at me and raised her eyebrows, "Well, I'm impressed."

"Don't be." I answered and quickly led her and Eryn to the deck. I grabbed some menus from one of the stations and we sat down under an awning. A server arrived with ice water.

"What can I get you to drink?"

Penn spoke up. "Bloody Mary for me."

"I'm good with water, thanks." I said.

"Same for me." Eryn nodded.

The server left. A few minutes later, Chuck walked out onto the deck. Looking more like a model despite the stains on his whites.

"Ladies, how are you today?" Penn perked up and batted her eyes at him.

"We are very well, thank you so much for taking time out of your busy schedule to welcome us."

I rolled my eyes. I suspect Eryn kicked Penn under the table. Chuck looked down at me.

"Are you on the clock?"

"Yes, Eryn's clock." I smiled sweetly back.

He laughed, "Fair enough. Have you decided what you would like to have today, or shall I surprise you?"

"Oh, I love surprises." Penn cooed.

"I'll have the shrimp salad plate." Eryn said.

"You can surprise me, too." I grinned.

"At least you'll be eating healthy today." He smiled and walked away.

"What was that about?" Eryn asked me.

"Oh, he just likes to make sure all his guests eat healthy." I shrugged it off, trying to avoid the explanation. I knew Eryn wasn't buying it, but she didn't want to have the conversation in front of Penn any more than I did. Especially with Penn flirting with Chuck the way she was. A short time later, lunch arrived via a server, and Penn was clearly disappointed. Chuck surprised us by sending out seared trout with asparagus. It was amazing, as always. When the server returned, I requested a piece of carrot cake to go so I could offer it to Tammi. As we were leaving, Chuck caught up with us. "Sarah, do you have a minute?"

"Sure," I turned to Eryn, "I'll be right there."

"Take your time."

I stepped to the side with Chuck. "Thank you for lunch, it was superb."

He nodded, "You doing, okay?"

I smiled. "I am. Really, I am."

"I'm worried about you."

I wasn't sure how to take that. Was he worried about me as a friend, an employee, something more?

"I appreciate that; it is nice to know someone worries about me." I smiled.

"I mean it."

"Me too." I gave him a serious look. "It makes it easier knowing that someone does care, and I can call if I need to."

"You absolutely can call me anytime."

"That makes you special." I said with all sincerity.

It was his turn to be speechless. I could tell he was trying to work out the meaning of my words.

"Listen, I have to get back; I left Tammi on her own on her second day. Thank you, for lunch and the dessert. I'm sure she will love it."

"You're welcome. Talk to you later," he said casually. It wasn't a question; it was as if it was a normal part of our day.

The girls were waiting. "What was that all about?" Penn asked, with an eye for deviousness.

"Just work stuff." I smiled and slid into the car.

The rest of the afternoon flew by smoothly. Tammi did indeed handle things nicely while we were gone and is a fan of carrot cake, so it all worked out.

Chapter 23
Chuck

The plans to expand were really coming together, although Sarah wasn't working full time yet. She worked at night from home, even though she wouldn't admit it. There was no way she was getting everything done on the weekends, and she refused to be paid for the time. The wedding was fast approaching, and she was stressing about it even though I keep reassuring her the reception will be perfect. I know she just wants everything to be right for Eryn and Blue. I do too. It is Blue's second marriage and I really want it to work for him this time.

Watching so many of my friends get their hearts broken by their high school sweethearts had left me jaded towards relationships. If a girl was okay with going out to the movies, a concert, or any other event, that was good with me as long as she understands there were no long-term commitments and the ones that got clingy got dismissed immediately. I would not put myself or frankly them through all that turmoil.

It was a slow Wednesday night when Blue came in for a drink. His bachelor party was coming up in a few days, and he wanted some down time before a night that would surely be a night to remember. I put the staff on notice not to disturb us unless it was an emergency.

Blue and I sat facing the water and having a beer.

"So, you've had a pretty busy week, huh?" Blue asked, referring to the attempted robbery.

"Well, it's been interesting."

"How's your staff holding up?"

"Pretty good, Brandon and Martha have been through it before, sad to say. I offered to pay for any counseling they wanted, neither of them has taken me up on the offer.

"What about Sarah?"

I stared into the water, the sinking sun and coming twilight turning it into an inky black.

"She is hard to figure out."

"How so?"

"She says she's fine. But I'm sure there is something more going on with her."

Blue nodded, "she's had a rough year, it could be that it is starting to pile up on her."

"I drove her home the night of the robbery, and once we got to her apartment, she asked me to take her someplace else. She didn't need to be alone, and she didn't want to be in her apartment."

"That's interesting."

"She called Penn but couldn't reach her. She was going to call Eryn, but I offered her my spare room, and she took me up on it."

Blue gave me the kind of look that says, 'I can't believe you did that.'

"It was all completely professional. She slept upstairs in the guest room I stayed downstairs, mostly."

"Mostly?"

"I fell asleep on the sofa and woke up to her screaming. She was having a night terror. I sat with her the rest of the night, again purely platonic."

"Are you sure? I mean, you were her knight in shining armor twice in one night."

"Yeah, I know, but I'm telling you it is not like that. It is something else. Something I can't put my finger on, and I care about her. I mean really care about her and it is really freaking me out."

Blue turned to face me, and he leaned forward with his elbows on his knees.

"I really don't have to tell you not to go messing with this girl's head, do I?"

"No! And why do you assume I mess with any woman's head?"

"Because you're a big handsome lug, and girls go for that type and then when you don't want to be serious, they get their hearts broken."

"If they get their heart broken, it is because they didn't listen. I am very upfront about my thoughts on relationships, and I make it very clear."

"Yeah, and every woman believes she can change a man." Blue took a pull from his beer.

"Anyway, this isn't like that."

"Have you given her the no attachments speech?"

"No, because there is no reason to, there isn't anything there but a working relationship."

"But you just said you cared about her." Blue pegged me with a hard stare.

"Yes, I did. And I do. But she doesn't know that."

"Really, do you honestly believe that?"

I looked at Blue for a minute, trying to decipher the question.

"You are keeping your feelings in check, but you let her spend the night at your house, you stay with her at her apartment after a bender with Penn, you check on her to ensure she is eating every day, and it's just professional?" Blue laughed and drained his beer. "How do you find the time to cook while texting all of your employees to make sure they ate a decent lunch?"

Blue's tone belied the smile on his face. I could tell he was not happy about the situation.

"How do you know...?"

"Because Sarah told Eryn and Eryn told me."

"Really?"

"Yeah, really, so listen to me carefully. Eryn is very protective of Sarah, like a little sister or something. Therefore, I am protective of her for Eryn. Don't screw this up."

"Dude, we've been through a hell of a lot together, and I'd walk through fire for you. But, on this one. I need you to stay out of it."

"Fair enough." Blue turned back to stare at the water, "just so long as we both know where we stand."

I nodded. Blue and I had been friends, no brothers, for so long there was no way a woman, not even Sarah, would come between us. But I also would not take any crap off of him either. Yes, I had feelings, very strong ones for Sarah. I wasn't sure if she had the same feelings for me, but we were professionals and we could handle working together. We could even be friends. I didn't consider what I did for Sarah any more than I would do for any other employee. I just didn't have any other employees that needed that kind of attention at the present time.

At least that is what I was telling myself.

I decided I needed to change the subject. "You ready for Friday night?"

Blue chuckled, "Sure, a bunch of drunk marines on a party boat, what could go wrong? Please remember I am the police chief and I do not need my face plastered all over the news in some bachelor party gone wild scenario."

"Don't worry, I have everything under control."

"Yeah, that is what I am afraid of."

Chapter 24
Sarah

The wedding was only days away now, and I think Penn and I were more nervous than Eryn.

We were planning a bachelorette party, which wouldn't differ from every other weekend when Penn, Eryn and I went out. Although Penn swears, she had something special planned, and Eryn threatened her under penalty of pain that it better not be something crazy and wild with male strippers. Penn assured us that will not be the case. But she won't even tell me what she has planned, so I'm worried.

I hadn't heard from Chuck all day, but then I imagined he is probably getting ready for Blue's party Friday night. Knowing some of their buddies from the Marine Corps were flying in for the wedding and the party, I wasn't surprised, though. Then I berated myself for being so selfish to think Chuck would consider spending time with me over his friends. We had a professional relationship. Okay, maybe it was a friendly sort of professional relationship, but still I had not shared my feelings about him, so what did I expect?

I got through the day at work in a haze and with little enthusiasm. When five o'clock came, I didn't waste any time getting in my car and driving home.

I told myself I was looking forward to a quiet night. No working late, no going out with the girls, just me and the movie channel. I was going to enjoy a frozen pizza and wine while watching some sappy romance movie. It was my thing, and I would not be ashamed of it. I kicked off my shoes and threw myself across my bed. I was trying to decide if I should soak in a hot tub of bubbles with a magazine before watching my movie. Or watch the movie and go to bed early and try to get some sleep?

I stripped and took a shower. I wrapped my hair in a towel afterwards and put on some flannel pajamas and my big fuzzy slippers. Then I sat on the bed and brushed out my damp hair. Next, I headed to the kitchen to retrieve a frozen pepperoni pizza and pop it in the oven while searching for an appropriately sappy movie to fit my mood.

As luck would have it, there was a rerun of a Christmas movie about a man and a woman snowbound in a ski resort that neither of them wanted to be at. They argue and bicker and then eventually fall in love.

The timer went off, so I ran to the kitchen, grabbed two slices of pizza on a plate and a glass of wine. I plopped down on the sofa just in time as the opening credits were rolling. Perfection.

Two more slices of pizza and another glass of wine later, and the movie was over; I was sleepy. Perhaps I would get some sleep after all. I left the plate and the glass in the sink and padded to bed.

I woke up to the sound of my phone announcing a text message.

I reached for it with barely one eye open, assuming it was from Penn.

"Can't go out, now." I text back, barely able to see the screen.

A reply came back, but I didn't bother to read it. I was too tired. Fumbling, I tried to put the phone back on the charger, but it fell to the floor. It didn't matter; it was late, and I dozed off. I woke up breathless and my heart racing from a dream of Chuck being shot by the robber. I needed something to drink, so I stumbled to the kitchen for water. While I was standing there, I heard knocking at the door. I froze. I wasn't sure what time it was, but it had to be late. Fear bloomed in the pit of my stomach, and I tiptoed to the door and looked out the peephole.

It was Chuck. I opened the door without a care as to the fact that I was still in my flannel pajamas and my hair had to be a disaster.

"Chuck, what are you doing here?"

"You sent me a message repeating my name. I thought you might be in trouble or something." He said, looking around the apartment.

"I've been asleep; I'm sorry I don't understand what you are talking about."

"Where's your phone?"

"Uh, maybe in the bedroom?" I retreated in search of the phone confused by Chuck's behavior. I looked around and finally found it under the bed.

"Here, it is!" I called out.

Chuck came to stand in the doorway. "May I?" He extended his hand.

"Sure." I handed him the phone.

"See here." He turned so we could both see the screen. I sent you a text, and you answered and then the mic must have gotten turned on."

I looked at the screen as the wave of embarrassment rolled up from my feet to crash into my cheeks.

"I was really asleep and must have hit the button when I was trying to get the phone back on the charger. I thought it was Penn texting me."

"I was worried you were being hurt or something."

"I..., well.... I had a bad dream about you getting shot, so that must have been it." My face had surpassed all shades of red and gone into purple at this point.

"Sarah, if you are having nightmares about the robbery you need to talk to someone." He handed me back my phone.

"And say what?"

"Tell someone how you feel about the situation; tell them about the nightmares."

I shook my head. "I talk to you."

He stood staring at me for a moment, as if he wasn't sure what to say next. So, I tried to defuse the situation as best I could.

"Listen, I am really, really sorry that this happened, and you came all the way over here in the middle of the night. I am beyond mortified." Tears of embarrassment stung my eyes, and I looked away.

"I was up anyway, and it is only midnight."

"Why don't we go make you some tea and set the reset button on your night."

"I don't think I have chamomile tea." I said, following him back to the kitchen.

"Do you have milk?"

"Hmm, maybe?"

"Sarah, I am going to set you up with home delivery of some fresh dairy and produce, you...." He turned and saw the empty frozen pizza box I had left on the counter.

I tried to pretend like it was no big deal. "Oh, sorry, the kitchen is a mess. I just wasn't in the mood to be tidy tonight." I rushed about, grabbing the box and putting it in the trash and rinsing the glass and dish in the sink before attempting to put them in the dishwasher.

"Sarah, Sarah, be still for a moment." Chuck took me by the shoulders.

I couldn't bring myself to look up at him.

He stood for a moment and waited. When I didn't move either, he took one hand and smoothed my hair.

"My hair, oh my god!" I cried.

"Sarah."

"I need to go change." I tried to turn away.

"Sarah." Chuck looked deeply into my eyes, "listen to me, you look fine."

"No! This is ridiculous, you've seen me hung over and now this." I was working myself up to a good hissy fit, "I'm probably going to quit; how can you work with someone who you see in their pajamas all the time?"

"Whoa! Hang on now, let's take it down a notch." He was still holding my shoulders. "Look at me, come on, look at me."

I raised my eyes to his.

"Just take a deep breath." He inhaled through his nose. He held his breath until I did the same.

He nodded, "Now exhale."

I blew out a breath.

"Do it again."

"Chuck."

He gave me a stare that said breathe or else. So, I inhaled.

"Close your eyes."

I did.

"Exhale."

I did as he said.

"Better? Good."

"Now, to answer your question, tons of people work together who have seen each other in their pajamas."

"Oh, really? Like whom?"

"Husband and wives that run restaurant businesses together." He grinned.

"Okay, true. But... wait what?" I wasn't sure I heard him correctly, or perhaps I did, but didn't understand his meaning.

"I'm just saying," he took a half step closer to me. "That there are lots of couples who live and work together as a team."

My mouth was suddenly dry. "What couples?" I whispered.

"Oh, just the kind that start out as friends and then grow into something more. I mean, a good relationship and an excellent team are essentially the same thing. Two people who trust each other and understand what the other person needs or wants."

I wanted to agree, but I had completely lost the ability to speak. I kept telling myself that I was wrong, that I was reading too much into his words. That I was letting my feelings for Chuck color everything he was saying to me.

"Does it sound like us?" He asked.

"Not exactly." I answered.

He looked disappointed.

"I mean, the big difference here is that I have never seen you in your pajamas."

"Oh, well." He stepped closer, and his hands moved from my shoulders up my neck to cradle my face as he leaned in. His lips hovering just above mine. "That's because I don't wear any."

Just as I sucked in a breath of shock, he gently brushed his warm, velvety lips across mine.

My mind was reeling. What was happening? Was I still dreaming? This couldn't be real. I leaned into him a little and he took the cue and kissed me a little more deeply. This time his tongue traced my lips ever so slightly. An involuntary moan escaped me, and I wrapped my arms around his neck.

When he pulled away, I opened my eyes to find him staring deeply at me.

"Chuck." I whispered.

"Sarah." He traced my jawline with his thumb. "I care for you in a way I have never cared for anyone before."

I didn't know what to say. It wasn't a declaration of love, but it was certainly something.

"Chuck, I...."

He let his thumb caress my lips, silencing me.

"I need you to be safe." He said.

I nodded.

"Can I stay here with you tonight?" He asked.

My mouth dropped open.

"I'll sleep on the sofa, if that is better."

"Yes, no. I uh."

Chuck furrowed his brow at me.

"Yes, stay." I blurted, afraid he would assume I wanted him to leave, and that was the last thing I wanted.

He smiled at me and nodded. "Okay, let's see what we can do about you getting some sleep."

"Are you kidding me?" I looked at him in surprise. "You really believe I'm going to sleep now? I'm not going to sleep for days." I bit my lip, realizing I was saying too much.

Chuck grinned at me. "Really? And why is that?"

"I mean, you know, just that...."

He began tracing my jawline again, and I felt like I was going to melt into a puddle on the kitchen floor. This time when his forefinger reached my lips, I slipped it into my mouth. Chuck smiled down at me and paused. I sucked at his finger a little.

"Sarah, you're killing me." His voice was husky.

I kissed him showing him, I wanted more.

"Sarah, I'm trying very hard to be a gentleman."

"Maybe, I don't want a gentleman." I caressed the back of his neck, then traced his jawline this time.

He groaned loudly. "Think carefully about what you want here, Sarah. Because I'm in love with you and there is no changing that if we take this any farther.

"I don't want it to change. I don't want it to stop."

His eyes danced as I spoke, and I understood that tonight would change everything.

"I love you." I said, my lips brushing against his ear.

At that moment, my feet lost contact with the floor as Chuck lifted me in his arms and carried me to the bedroom.

Chapter 25
Sarah

I woke up early Sunday morning; I hadn't seen Chuck since Friday night. We both had wedding obligations, and I had got through Eryn's party Saturday night without having to tell Penn and Eryn that Chuck and I had slept together. There would be time to tell them about that later. Today was Eryn's big day, and Penn and I needed to focus on making sure everything was perfect for her.

I jumped out of bed and grabbed a shower; my dress was waiting for me at Penn's shop, along with Eryn's dress. Penn had arranged for us to have our hair and makeup done there. Once we were ready, a limo would take us to the wedding at the large gazebo, out at the old fort. It was a beautiful setting along the water, and a very popular wedding venue.

I rushed into the kitchen to make a little breakfast and had to smile to myself as I opened the fridge. Chuck had been true to his word, and a delivery of fresh fruits and vegetables had arrived yesterday. I popped a coffee pod into the machine while I put together a bowl of fruit and yogurt. My phone buzzed with a text from Chuck.

"Are you up?"

"Yes, having fresh fruit for breakfast."

"That's my girl."

"See you later today." I smiled. I was looking forward to seeing Chuck in his morning suit with the other groomsmen.

"See you later."

Chuck was Blue's best man and Penn was the maid of honor, so he would walk her down the aisle and one of Blue's other friends would escort me. But that was okay. I still got to stand across from the groomsmen and admire Chuck.

As I was washing out my bowl, my phone rang.

"Hello?"

"Sarah, it's Penn, are you ready?"

"I am."

"Okay, the car is on the way to pick you up."

"See you soon."

Penn had arranged for Eryn and me to be picked up and brought to the shop. When we arrived, she had fresh coffee, juice and croissants waiting. There was already a small army of people there ready to style our hair, apply makeup, and help us with our dresses.

"Are you nervous?" I asked Eryn as we settled into our chairs.

"A little."

"Now's the time to back out if you're getting cold feet." Penn advised.

"I don't have cold feet about marrying Blue, I just am a little nervous about doing it in front of a crowd."

"You won't even know we are there. Once you see Blue, you'll be so focused on him the rest of it will melt away." I tried to offer some comfort.

"I hope you're right."

Three hours later, we were ready. Eryn was stunning in her elegant sheath wedding dress. Penn had done an amazing job of designing the perfect dress to reflect Eryn's style.

The dresses Penn designed for us were a very pale blue. The color of the dresses allowed the blue and turquoise calla lilies we carried to stand out. Penn had arranged for a photographer to capture all the important moments of the day. There were a few pictures taken while we were having our hair and make-up done. Afterwards, we toasted one another with champagne and posed for more photos before climbing into the limo and driving out to Ft. Monroe. There was a small tent set up for Eryn to slip into in keeping with the tradition of not letting the groom see the bride before the ceremony. Eryn's father was waiting for her. Penn and I proceeded to the designated area to meet up with our escorts.

There was the police bagpiper standing by, ready to play the wedding march. It was a small crowd of family and friends. The sky was a beautiful blue; the weather was warm. Everything was picture perfect, as if Penn had commanded Mother Nature to cooperate. A second photographer appeared to ensure every magical moment was captured. A white limo waited to whisk Eryn and Blue to the restaurant for the reception; Penn and I would share our limo with the groomsmen and other attendees.

I looked around nervously and spotted Chuck. He was drop dead gorgeous in his suit; his hair slicked back. He gave me a little wink before turning his attention back to Penn. I ducked my head to hide the smile.

"Chuck's a great guy." My escort, Travis whispered.

I looked up in surprise.

He chuckled, "Please, you're all he talked about all weekend." Then he returned his gaze straight ahead as music played and it was time to start the ceremony.

Eryn was so beautiful walking down the aisle and up into the gazebo, and the look on Blue's face was priceless. I knew every woman there felt the same way I did. We all wanted a man to gaze at us the way Blue looked at Eryn at that moment. Then, just like that, the ceremony was over and Blue, and Eryn were whisked away. I was a little sad that I probably wouldn't get to talk to Eryn anymore today before she was left for her honeymoon and when she got back, I would be working for Chuck full time. My heart felt sad for what seemed like a loss while being happy for Eryn's new beginning at the same time.

"Come on, sweetie." Penn said gently as she guided me to our own limo.

"Sorry, I was just,"

"I know."

We climbed into the limo with the groomsmen, but Chuck wasn't there. The door closed, and the driver started the car.

"Wait, where's Chuck?" I asked.

"Oh, he left early to get to the restaurant to make sure everything was ready for Eryn and Blue when they got there." Travis answered.

"Oh."

"It'll be okay." He reassured me.

I wasn't sure exactly what he meant, but I had been looking forward to riding with Chuck to the reception. Then I wondered if I shouldn't have planned to go ahead as well, but it was too late for that. I hoped everything would be as perfect as the ceremony. I reached over and squeezed Penn's hand.

"You did a marvelous job today."

She looked at me and smiled. "Thank you."

I was certain she wanted to cry. As sad as I was, I'm sure Penn felt it even more since her, and Eryn having been besties for so long. Penn and I held hands on the way to the reception.

When we arrived, the guests were all in the front with drinks. Blue and Eryn should be in the back room closest to the deck, having a moment to themselves before the guests joined them. The rest of the wedding party and I would join them before the guests, many of whom were still arriving, would be shown to the reception room. No doubt the photographer was getting some pictures of the bride and groom.

Chapter 26
Chuck

I woke earlier than usual; It was the big day, and I wanted to make sure Blue, and the boys were free of any hangover symptoms before we had to be at the old fort for the wedding ceremony. None of us had really drank all that much, but we were all older now and sometimes it doesn't take much to get a headache or worse. I made coffee and started breakfast for those who had crashed at my place overnight, to include Blue. I needed him at his very best today.

Once the guys were up, fed, and cured of any hint of a hangover, we were on our way to the ceremony. Blue hadn't seen Eryn in two nights, and he was a nervous wreck. I hadn't seen Sarah since Friday night at her apartment and frankly; I wanted this day to be over so I could see her again. We wouldn't be able to spend much time together until much later, and it was killing me. I had feelings for Sarah since I met her, but that night in her apartment, I knew then she was the only person I wanted to share my life with. It was crazy because we had never even dated in the conventional sense, but who cares. No one dates like that anymore anyway, and I wanted this woman. I needed her, and I was going to make damn sure she knew it.

Everything leading up to the ceremony was great. We were all there on time; we were all properly dressed. I had the ring in my pocket. Then the limo arrived with Sarah, but I couldn't see her because they wanted to keep Eryn out of sight until the ceremony started, my heart was racing just knowing she was there.

Blue was standing with the minister. Travis and I were waiting for Penn and Sarah, and then I saw her step out from the tent. She was incredibly beautiful. I was a little unsteady on my feet for a moment, and Travis had to put his hand on my shoulder to steady me.

"Whoa there, big guy."

"I'm fine." I said or something like that. Sarah had enraptured me.

"She is beautiful." Travis stated.

"Yes, she is. She is the most beautiful creature on this earth." I heard Travis chuckle and remove his heavy hand.

"Stand tough, marine."

I straighten my spine and exhaled. I couldn't take my eyes off her. Suddenly, everything in the world made sense. All those sappy love songs on the radio. I finally got it. Poetry, I totally understand now why people write it. I looked up at the sky. Had it always been this blue, or was it just because Sarah was here to make it glow?

Her eyes searched for me, and she smiled when we made eye contact. I wanted to kiss her. But the music started, and Penn was at my side, and I had to turn away.

Once the ceremony started, everything was a blur. I had ridden my bike to the fort so that I could leave right after the "I do's" were over and make sure everything was set up.

The restaurant was a hive of activity, some guests who did not go to the ceremony were already there with more guests arriving every minute. I didn't even see Sarah when she came in, but a server told me they were ready for the entire wedding party in the back room. I had to return to my best man's duties.

As soon as I walked in the room, I spotted Sarah and again she took my breath away. The photographer was giving direction, so I'd have to wait to talk to her again. Then everyone was seated at the tables and the guests could enter.

There were toasts and speeches, and I couldn't wait for this to be over.

Finally, it was announced that the bride and groom were leaving to begin their honeymoon, and the guests rushed outside to wish them well. The white limo was idling in the parking lot to take Eryn and Blue to the hotel for the night before they caught their flight tomorrow. They weren't the only ones with plans for the night. Blue had loaned me his boat, and I had it tied up to the pier outback. Eryn and been kind enough to put some of her clothes on board for Sarah to change into later.

Finally, Eryn and Blue were gone. The guests filtered out, and the staff started cleaning up. It was early evening, and I couldn't wait to get Sarah alone. I found her talking to Eryn's father, and as I approached, he detached himself and moved away. Before Sarah could escape, I put my arm around her and whispered in her ear.

"I thought it was understood that the bride was to be the prettiest woman on her wedding day."

Sarah smiled and leaned into me. My heart raced.

"And I thought the groom was supposed to be the most handsome."

"Come on." I stepped back a little but kept my arm around her.

"Where are we going?"

"It's a surprise."

"Shouldn't we help clean up?"

"No." I said flatly.

"Chuck, really what is going on?"

"Do you trust me?"

"Of course, I do."

"Then stop asking questions and come with me." I pleaded.

"Okay."

Sarah took my hand and I lead her out to the pier.

"Is this Blue's boat?"

"It is, and he loaned it to us. Take off your shoes."

I stepped aboard and then lifted her across so she wouldn't ruin her dress. I threw off the lines, started the engine, and we trolled down the creek and out to the bay. I kept us close enough to the shore for navigation, but far away enough for privacy.

The water was calm, and the forecast was calling for clear skies and low only around sixty degrees. It was going to be a perfect night. At least that was my plan.

Once we got out into the water, I slowed the boat down and then found a pleasant spot to drop anchor.

"This is pretty." Sarah said, looking at the sunset.

"Yes, you are." I said, sounding corny as hell, but I didn't care, it was true.

She turned her face to me and smiled the smile that reaches her eyes and makes them crinkle in the corners in the most adorable way.

"So, what are we doing?" She asked again.

I was wondering how she would react to what I had planned for the evening.

"Sarah, I know this probably sounds a little crazy, but to me it couldn't be more right. I've loved you from the moment I laid eyes on you, and I tried to deny it to myself; to Blue, and to others who could see right through me. And I was afraid you didn't feel the same way about me. But now that I know you care for me the same way; I don't want to spend another moment of this life without you."

At that point, I dropped to one knee and pulled a second ring out of my pocket. "Sarah, will you marry me?"

Sarah stood looking down at me in shock and disbelief. I was kneeling in front of her, both of us still dressed in our wedding attire. She was holding my heart and my future in her hands.

"Yes."

I stared at her in disbelief, "Yes?"

She laughed and then cried. "Yes, Chuck, I'll marry you."

I carefully placed the ring on her finger, and then stood up and kissed her passionately.

"Sarah, I am going to spend every day for the rest of my life proving to you how much I love you."

I picked her up and spun her around. "I love you with all my heart."

She wrapped her arms around my neck, and I never wanted either of us to let go. I carried her below deck to the stateroom. I never knew what joy was until I knew I would spend the rest of my life with Sarah in my arms.

The End

Don't miss out!

Visit the website below and you can sign up to receive emails whenever Lynn Story publishes a new book. There's no charge and no obligation.

https://books2read.com/r/B-A-ULCK-AOMRB

BOOKS 2 READ

Connecting independent readers to independent writers.

Also by Lynn Story

A Gates Point Novel
Rescue My Love
The Primrose Heart

A Gates Point Novel
Rescue My Love
Ginny's Christmas Wish
Love at Bay
The Primrose Heart
Love at Bay
Her Private Chef

Watch for more at www.stitchesandstories.com.

About the Author

Lynn is a native of the Hampton Roads region of Virginia, the area which is the inspiration for the Gates Point series. She enjoys time in, on and around the Chesapeake Bay and its tributaries. When she isn't out exploring, she enjoys spending time at home with her husband in the garden.

Read more at www.stitchesandstories.com.

www.ingramcontent.com/pod-product-compliance
Lightning Source LLC
Chambersburg PA
CBHW030548030726
47495CB00004B/1177